**Previous seasons in the
Peter Owen World Series**

Season 1: Slovenia
Evald Flisar, *Three Loves, One Death*
Jela Krečič, *None Like Her*
Dušan Šarotar, *Panorama*

Season 2: Spain (Castilian)
Cristina Fernández Cubas, *Nona's Room*
Julio Llamazares, *Wolf Moon*
José Ovejero, *Inventing Love*

OTHER TITLES IN THE WORLD SERIES SERBIAN SEASON

Filip David, *The House of Remembering and Forgetting* (translated by Christina Pribichevich Zorić)

Mirjana Novaković, *Fear and His Servant* (translated by Terence McEneny)

PETER OWEN WORLD SERIES

'*The world is a book, and those who do not travel read only one page,*' wrote St Augustine. Journey with us to explore outstanding contemporary literature translated into English for the first time. Read a single book in each season – which will focus on a different country or region every time – or try all three and experience the range and diversity to be found in contemporary literature from across the globe.

Read the world – three books at a time

3 works of literature in
2 seasons each year from
1 country each season

For information on forthcoming seasons go to peterowen.com / istrosbooks.com

THE TRAGIC FATE OF MORITZ TÓTH

Dana Todorović

THE TRAGIC FATE OF MORITZ TÓTH

*Translated from the Serbian by
the author*

PETER OWEN
WORLD SERIES

WORLD SERIES SEASON 3 : SERBIA
THE WORLD SERIES IS A JOINT INITIATIVE BETWEEN
PETER OWEN PUBLISHERS AND ISTROS BOOKS

Peter Owen Publishers / Istros Books
Conway Hall, 25 Red Lion Square, London WC1R 4RL, UK

Peter Owen and Istros Books are distributed in the USA and Canada by
Independent Publishers Group/Trafalgar Square
814 North Franklin Street, Chicago, IL 60610, USA

Translated from the Serbian *Tragična sudbina Morica Tota*

Copyright © Dana Todorović 2008
English translation copyright © Dana Todorović 2017

All Rights Reserved.
No part of this publication may be reproduced in any form or by any means without the written permission of the publishers.

The moral rights of the author and translator are hereby asserted in accordance with the Copyright Designs and Patents Act 1988.

Paperback ISBN   978-0-7206-1983-6
Epub ISBN   978-0-7206-1984-3
Mobipocket ISBN   978-0-7206-1985-0
PDF ISBN   978-0-7206-1986-7

A catalogue record for this book is available from the British Library.

Cover design: Davor Pukljak, frontispis.hr
Typeset by Octavo Smith Publishing Services

Printed by Printfinder, Riga, Latvia

Part One

The first opera I ever saw was Puccini's *Turandot*. In fact, the circumstances in which I found myself before this staged musical spectacle were entirely unusual, and this is the story of how it all occurred.

I remember well that it happened in wintertime – more precisely, during that unfortunate winter following that unfortunate autumn following that unfortunate summer when Juliska departed this world. One morning in that unfortunate winter I received an unexpected call from Marika Földes of the local Employment Office. She informed me that a rather interesting job offer had come up and that I should present myself in exactly two hours and forty minutes at the main entrance of the Hungarian State Opera House, where a certain Mr Kis would be waiting for me. She did not wish to impart any further details regarding the nature of the proposition over the phone since, as she explained, she was in a rush to get to a meeting and also felt that Mr Kis was far more competent to discuss the issue.

I had waited a long time to receive any news from the Employment Office, so not following up on the invitation was hardly an option. I arrived at the bus station, and by the time I took notice of the bus to Budapest parked at Platform 12, the driver had already started the engine, so I had no choice but to break into a sprint. The bus started to move as soon as I got on, and I barely managed to scramble to an empty seat. I remember finding a place in the second-to-last row, next to a scowling adolescent. Not having the slightest idea what to expect upon reaching my destination, I sought comfort in what seemed to be the only certainty at the time – the monotonous route of the intercity bus line, nestled in the softness of my well-worn foam seat and the familiar, stale smell of old metal. This must have been how I dozed off – to the soporific rumble of the engine – and when I woke up and glanced out the window I was greeted by a view of lazy winter clouds descending towards the village roofs, set against the backdrop of the snowy hills of Buda.

Mr Kis was most certainly *kis*, the Hungarian for 'small'. He sported a brown trench coat with a raised collar and a black hat, and he kept his hands firmly in his pockets. His hat, being about two sizes too big, had fallen over his eyes, causing him to tilt his head back in order to see. When I spotted him as I was waiting for the light to turn green on the opposite side of the street, he was nervously shifting his weight from foot to foot and scrutinizing his surroundings in a seemingly clandestine manner, probably trying to single me out in the crowd of passers-by. His conspiratorial behaviour and appearance suddenly revealed before my eyes an entire range of possibilities as to the upcoming job offer – black-market dealer, drug smuggler, pimp, hit man – for the real nature of the offer could end up differing entirely from the information available to the Employment Office. Not knowing quite how to act, I continued to stand there as the light turned green twice and all the other pedestrians energetically passed by me. This is when Kis noticed me, and just as I felt my cheeks burning with shame and was about to finally start walking away the little green man in the traffic light once again invited me to cross the street.

To my relief, the introduction was direct and painless. Kis made only one comment through his crooked smirk – a comment I was very much accustomed to and had even expected – that this was not at all how he had imagined me. He then suggested that we continue our conversation at the café adjacent to the Opera House.

As it happened, we hardly spoke a word during the first ten minutes of our acquaintance. Just as we were about to sit down, Kis's mobile phone started ringing, and he hurried to the doorway, excusing himself with gesticulations referring to the bad signal inside. This gave me more than enough time to think of a few plausible excuses for declining his generous offer. 'I live in a small town, you see . . . what would the neighbours say if they found out . . . last year was particularly difficult for me, and I hardly managed to keep myself on an even keel . . .' However, the explanation he provided when he returned to the table proved the offer to be surprisingly benign and socially acceptable. As coordinator of the *Turandot* project, scheduled to première a few days later in the main concert hall of the Opera House, it was his duty to find someone who would 'feed' the main tenor his lines while positioned in the left wing between the stage and the orchestra pit – in other words, to act as a prompter. A flood of relief came over me. He explained that they did not generally use prompters but that the tenor in the role of Calaf had fallen ill with jaundice and his replacement appeared to be afflicted with certain 'cognitive difficulties' – as Kis had gently put it. During the same evening I had the opportunity to observe that the man was, in fact, such a dunce that he couldn't memorize half of his lines. Rumour had it – as I happened to overhear a couple of days later at dress rehearsal in a conversation between the second violinists and a talkative harpist during rests between musical phrases – that the director Lajos Gorzowski, a pompous eccentric, was particularly impressed with the singer's audition since 'his oral presentation managed to bring him to the highest degree of bliss' and that it was this particular skill that ultimately got him hired.

When I asked him why they didn't opt for a professional prompter, Kis explained that the Hungarian Union of Prompters had begun an active boycott a few months earlier against the management of a number of theatres in town and that they refused to work under conditions that did not meet their unrealistically high standards. What Kis meant by 'conditions' became clear to me when I arrived for the rehearsal at five forty-five on the same day and became acquainted with my planned workspace.

The prompter was supposed to sit in a small, rudimentary wooden box which the director – ignoring a perfectly capable team of set designers – had built with his own hands only a day before. Gorzowski, incidentally, was a very enterprising man who, like many who consider themselves artists, took pleasure in meddling in the jobs of others, convinced that it placed him in total control of the project. The reason for such unconventional positioning of the prompter, as was explained to me, was the equally unconventional and ultra-sophisticated method of lighting that would later prove to be responsible for the show's immense popularity – because of the way the light was designed to be reflected, a prompter standing behind the curtain or sitting in a conventional prompt-box would cast the shadow of a human figure on stage. The only possible solution was to include the prompter in the set itself, and given that the opera takes place on the grounds of the exotic Imperial Palace in Beijing, the set designers had come up with the idea of covering the box with a piece of ivory-coloured wallpaper and placing a prominent oriental statue on top, thus disguising it as a kind of pedestal.

The claustrophobic tightness of the box was alleviated only by a tiny opening through which I was supposed to whisper the lines to the good-for-nothing Calaf. Seeing the box for the first time, after I was informed that I, Moritz Tóth, was expected to squat inside it twice a week for 2,140 forints an hour, I cursed the day I handed over the form to Marika Földes in the Employment Office in Etyeki Street. The thought that my financial standing did not allow me to refuse the offer, whatever it may be, only amplified my frustration. To make matters worse, when I received the text I discovered that it was in Italian, which should have been obvious had I not overlooked the fact amid all the confusion. That I couldn't speak a word of Italian was of little concern to my employers. They told me to read it as it was written – exactly as I would were the text in Hungarian. 'The main purpose of the prompter is to stimulate the memory of the performer, and the precision with which the lines are pronounced is of secondary importance,' were the exact words of the assistant director. I remember feeling as if I had wandered off into some distorted version of reality where the boundaries between possible and impossible either don't exist or surpass my understanding. I also remember having spent that entire night repeating Calaf's lines under my dim kitchen light, peering at the text until my eyes became bloodshot, conscious of the fact that the dress rehearsal was only two days away.

As the dress rehearsal approached I became more and more anxious. I was expected at the Opera by six forty-five, but I arrived as early as at ten to six, when there was no one but a security guard to greet me. The man checked my ID and attached a laminated pass to my lapel, after which I was set free to roam the corridors of the Opera House and admire the impressively decorated interior, the remarkable marble columns, the colourful frescos of Greek gods by painter Károly Lotz. Curiosity compelled me to penetrate deeper into the building and explore the back corridors. At one point I peeped into a room from which I could hear cheerful chattering and caught sight of a costume assistant measuring the chest circumference of a scantily clad girl – most likely an extra – beside a massive mirror. I continued to walk down the corridors and penetrate deeper into the building until I finally stopped at the sight of the room capable of evoking in me a deep feeling of nostalgia – the orchestra room.

There was nobody inside. The instruments were neatly resting in their places, and the music scores stood on the stands, open to the middle of the dynamic third act. In a world so unfamiliar to me, the image was pure comfort to my soul. I quietly entered, picked up a violin bow and realized that some fifteen years had passed since I had last held a bow in my hands. My fingertips glided over the strings, and my thoughts drifted to my childhood . . . it seemed for a few seconds that I was sitting on a suitcase back in Moscow's Pushkin Square, watching my grandfather, the master of improvisation, courageously dive into trills and fly through arpeggios, leaving bystanders breathless . . . But my recollection was cut short by voices from the hallway. Without delay, I placed the bow back to its original position, scurried out of the room, barely managing to avoid an onslaught of self-confident and talkative musicians advancing towards the orchestra room as I veered around the corner.

I wandered the corridors a while longer, watching the excitement around me grow as voices and sounds gradually filled every nook of the impressive interior. About a half-hour later, in the midst of preparations, the assistant manager – a likable young man with a gigantic collection of keys at his belt – dashed by and acknowledged me with a hearty slap on the shoulder. This small gesture of attention later proved to be his universal sign of encouragement, but at the time I took it to mean only one thing – that the moment had come for the dress rehearsal.

In this performance, the ice princess Turandot was to be portrayed by the magnificent Erzsébet Szántó, now in the prime of her career. Decorated with an embroidered oriental motif, her long black gown must have been supported by a hefty wire frame around her body, since her movements could not be detected in the slightest as she gracefully descended the wide stairway of the palace and headed towards the stage like a floating apparition. Her face was covered with a fine silk veil, yet something behind that veil seemed to radiate and allude to her unusual beauty. As I watched her in utter admiration during the first act of the dress rehearsal, I had no way of knowing that in the final act that same veil would be torn to shreds right before my eyes, revealing her flawless and luminous complexion and soft Botticellian facial features in contrast to her expressive eyes and a soft gaze that seemed as if it could melt the thickest of ice floes.

Indeed, it was Erzsébet Szántó who captivated me during the final act and achieved the impossible – to awaken in me an unrelenting inclination towards opera as an artistic form. The final act of *Turandot* was my first glimpse at what would later become my greatest passion, perpetuated in everything I did thereafter. To put it simply, I was hooked. I ached for more, and this new yearning seemed instantly to take precedence over all other concerns, including my benumbed knees, the inappropriately restricted work space, Mr Kis and Gorzowski's sexual inclinations.

From that moment on the infamous wooden box assumed particular importance, as it became my most sacred hiding place and at the same time a bitter reminder of a life I would never get to taste and a kind of love I would never again experience. Calaf knew most of the popular librettos by heart, allowing me time to wander off into a world far more exciting than the one I knew. Crouching in the confined space, hidden from all eyes and judgement, I would quietly sing 'Nessun Dorma' to the ice princess with a Hungarian phonetic undertone, imagining that I was the one whose kiss – as the plot instructs – would reveal to her a secret so powerful it brought all the people of Beijing to their feet.

Chamber C of the Second Wing was much plainer in appearance than Tobias had previously imagined, and the fact that it was vacant upon his arrival allowed him to observe it in its most genuine of states, divorced from the presence of people and their multitude of dispositions and inclinations.

How strange it is – thought Tobias as he took a few cautious steps around – that time has turned this room into something of a myth. Demagogues persistently ranted about it, officials exchanged dark jokes about it during breaks in the hallways, children chewed it up in tongue-twisters and it even entered into curses: May your mother have to spend days sweeping up pieces of you in Chamber C of the Second Wing! Yet, hardly anyone had any notion of what it actually looked like – there were only a handful of such people – and when Tobias stepped across its threshold that morning, to his misfortune he became one of them. However, this did not turn out to be Tobias's greatest misfortune at the time. His greatest misfortune at that precise moment was that under the agreeable impression as to the surprisingly plain appearance of Chamber C, he somehow managed to suppress all other feelings and apprehensions.

Ever since he had been informed that disciplinary proceedings were initiated against him and that he would be put on the stand in Chamber C of the Second Wing, not for a single moment did Tobias deny that he had committed the act for which he was charged – moreover, he was proud of it and spoke about it openly, and under no circumstances would he have considered it a wrongdoing. He believed that the act he had committed was a virtuous deed at the very least. At the moment of perpetration he was more than aware of the consequences he may face as a result, but he saw it as an endeavour worth the risk and felt great pride in mustering the courage to perform a deed that placed the interests of another before his own.

Hence, when he set foot in the notorious room, the sight before his eyes invoked in him a flicker of hope, a new wave of optimism that perhaps the situation was not as black and unequivocal as would be expected and that the Disciplinary Committee would realize the true nature of his deed. At the same time he disregarded any thoughts about what his existence would amount to should they decide to impose the penalty; a thing he had feared only a moment before.

At my new place of employment I became known as 'the Red Priest', but soon enough the nickname was shortened simply to 'Priest'. At first I didn't dare ask what this nickname alluded to but had decided to accept it unconditionally, presuming it to be some sort of a humorous reference in the world of classical music that I'd better not question openly, particularly considering that I was new at the Opera. Then, on one lazy Saturday afternoon at the book fair, I stumbled upon a book in English called *Vivaldi: The Red Priest of Venice*. Not in my wildest dreams could I afford such a luxury (the book cost a staggering 7,320 forints!), but I managed to convince the shop assistant to translate the entire preface by leading her to believe that I had serious intentions of purchasing it.

This is when I discovered that the Red Priest, that is *Il Prete Rosso*, had been the nickname of the legendary Italian violinist and composer Antonio Vivaldi on account of his flaming red hair and the fact that he had briefly studied to become a priest. As a hardcore punk, I owed my flaming red hair not to genetics but to a tube of Koleston hair dye of the shade 77/44, and my wardrobe at the time consisted of scruffy woollen sweaters stretched down to the knees and black T-shirts dedicated to the Funeral, Stairway to Hell and Filthy Communion. In conjunction with this, I sported outlandish fashion accessories, such as a pair of thick safety pins in each ear and a BMX bicycle chain around my neck.

Filthy Communion was the name of the punk band in which I played during my late adolescent years. There were four of us in the group, Izsák Gaál on bass, Bodi Mészáros on drums, Attila Varga, the lead vocalist, and my humble self, Moritz Tóth, on guitar. Be it justified or not, we proudly harboured the conviction that our musical style could be defined as a cross between the Sex Pistols and the Dead Kennedys, with aesthetic elements of horror-punk borrowed from the Misfits and expressed through an ultra-eccentric style of dress and makeup. Like all other anonymous bands, we performed in cheap local joints, at student events and minor socio-political protests. We had a following of anarchistic high-school kids and misunderstood philosophy and art students, although our gigs were never complete without the presence of some impoverished layabout who would stop by for the cheap beer and end up sleeping face down on the podium.

My beginnings in the provocative musical movement and subculture of punk were marked by the moment I sold the violin my grandfather gave me for my fifth birthday and traded it for an incomparably cheaper used electric Ibanez. Having already been so well acquainted with a stringed instrument, I mastered the guitar in a flash. Nonetheless, I had to be extremely skilful to hide my business transaction and newly discovered passion for the guitar from my grandfather, knowing his heart would split in two if he found out I had sold my violin. And keeping this secret was no easy task, considering that I lived with him in a forty-square-metre, one-bedroom flat.

My grandfather was a member of a highly successful travelling

Gypsy ensemble called Honey Cakes. Rumour had it that during some festive get-together the ensemble's double bass player was so impressed by my grandfather's virtuoso skills and daring improvisations that he got down on his knees and begged him to join them on their upcoming tour, which was how my grandfather became the first non-Roma member in the history of the ensemble. He would often take me along on tour to Romania, Austria, even Russia. Looking back, I can safely say that I had spent the most memorable moments of my childhood on the pavements of central-European capitals as well as on shabby wool blankets in front of crackling fires, immersed in the aroma of warm bread and the pleasing sound of cimbaloms.

The repercussions of my failed attempt to hide the guitar from my grandfather surfaced on one cold January evening – I recall that the streets still quivered from the dim glimmer of dying Christmas lights. I had returned home from my afternoon classes to find my grandfather seated at the dining-room table with an unusual, almost remote sadness in his eyes. In contrast, his violin shone with contentment behind the glass double door of the china cabinet. I had an instant visual of the events that had taken place, and the feeling of guilt that came over me at that very moment has lingered to this very day. What had happened was that my grandfather decided to reward his violin for its many years of service with a good polish. He had intended to do the same with mine, but my instrument was nowhere to be found, and in its usual place, under the bed in my room, stood a bizarre electric device connected by cable to a glaring red guitar.

My grandfather and I never spoke a word about it. At the time my adolescent mind accepted his decision to remain silent as an alleviating circumstance, but the event would later cast a shadow of distrust on our relationship, while the memory of it would come back to haunt me in my later years.

I have permitted myself this short digression into childhood in order to truthfully depict the emotion that crept up on me when, after all those years, I tentatively took his violin out of the dust-covered suitcase, guided by the profound impression that the opera *Turandot* had left on me. I held my grandfather's most precious possession in my sweat-soaked hands, which trembled as though the instrument were made of the most delicate of crystals. I gently placed my jaw on the chin rest of the violin, and for the first time in fifteen years I hesitantly drew the bow over the strings. Only a fleeting moment later, I could feel my heart ascend to the first few measures of Sarasate's *Gypsy Airs*.

'Your name?'

These were the Presiding Officer's first words to Tobias. His voice was rather thin for such a large man, and Tobias suspected that he was burdened with something of an orthodontic anomaly, as he spoke with a certain impediment, causing missiles of saliva to shoot across the room at random targets.

'Tobias Keller,' he answered.

'What is it that you do, Mr Keller?'

'I am the Adviser for Moral Issues with the Office of the Great Overseer.'

'I see. That would –'

'A philosopher . . .' mumbled the Prosecutor, who was seated to the side, his gaze fixed on a willowy woman with a yellowish complexion and large round glasses, who had taken notice of him upon his bombastic entrance and in whom he recognized an excellent opportunity to gain the sympathies of the Disciplinary Committee.

'Mr Diodorus, what gives you the right to interrupt me?' the Presiding Officer asked sternly.

The Prosecutor started, surprised that the Presiding Officer was able to hear his quiet remark, then flashed a wide grin to both him and the members of the Committee.

'Forgive me, sir, but I couldn't resist conveying my modest impressions to the charming lady in the reseda-green dress. You may rest assured it will not happen again.'

The yellowish complexion of the woman with the round glasses suddenly turned pink, and she looked away from the Prosecutor.

'I'm glad to hear it,' said the Presiding Officer and took a thick bundle of documents out of his drawer. He rummaged through the bundle until he finally pulled out what he had been looking for.

'I shall now deliver the opening statement of this hearing,' he began in an official tone.

'The defendant Tobias Keller is charged with committing the criminal act described under Article 98a of the Causal Authority Regulations, the reasons being that at six fifty a.m. on 12 March of the present year he connected the Extraordinary Activity Device to the faculty of his free will, and, having observed over the monitor a set of circumstances on the scene which would allow him to carry out his plan, he set a trap for the cyclist in the form of a sizeable egg-shaped pebble, after which the cyclist abruptly veered off his path in an attempt to avoid the above-mentioned pebble and sped towards the hydraulic digger that was advancing from the opposite direction, thus causing a sequence of events with the purpose of involving an intermediary in order to exert an unanticipated influence on the subject, i.e. Moritz Tóth, as the final destination on the path of influence, that is to say . . .'

At this point the Presiding Officer paused, cast a superficial glance over the text that followed and, realizing that there was more than he had expected, uttered, 'Well, I don't see the need to preoccupy ourselves with the details . . . I imagine you all skimmed through the material that was handed out prior to this hearing.'

The members of the Committee nodded in unison.

'In that case,' said the Presiding Officer, significantly deepening his voice as if to emphasize the importance and weight of his words, 'the key question that now lies before us is . . .'

The Presiding Officer paused then spoke directly to Tobias. 'Mr Keller, did you commit the act I had just described?'

'I did, sir.'

The Presiding Officer was visibly confused by Tobias's affirmative response, which, in turn, puzzled Tobias, since he had already noticed that his confession to the inspector was among the documents on the Presiding Officer's desk. The Presiding Officer needed a few moments to gather his thoughts.

'Good . . . or, shall I say, excellent! The identification of the perpetrator is of vital importance to the disciplinary proceedings!'

The obsequious Prosecutor compliantly nodded at the words of the Presiding Officer, who was gazing around the room, clearly indecisive as to the further course of the proceedings.

A strange sort of silence followed, which to Tobias seemed to last an eternity in the presence of this bizarre group of people. The Presiding Officer kept fidgeting in his chair and producing guttural sounds that were presumably supposed to aid his thinking process, until he unexpectedly broke the silence by hitting his palms resolutely on the desk and concluding, 'In that case, we shall take a short twenty-minute recess.'

One by one they all left the room – the Presiding Officer being the last among them as lifting such a massive weight off a chair was no easy task – while the dispirited Tobias simply remained slumped in his seat. Even though he was left alone once again, Chamber C of the Second Wing no longer seemed that empty.

It was three and a half months later, as the first blush of morning rose over the town, when I first took notice of that dreadful creature. I had risen early so that I could practise a technically demanding ascending sequence on my violin in the absence of the squeal of the old tram tracks and the jovial voices of children. I liked to practise right next to the window, under the delicate morning light, and this is where he caught my eye. He was leaning on a birch tree in front of number thirteen on the opposite side of the street, gazing in my direction. The reason I have chosen the words 'in my direction' is because I was not entirely sure whether he was looking at me in particular or if it was something else that was holding his attention – in fact, I wasn't even sure he'd seen me.

Odd in appearance, he was a rather chinless creature, with a beaky nose and a pair of peculiar, abnormally large eyes. Even though his hair was predominantly thinning, its remaining long strands, the colour of ash, danced wildly above his head in the wind, as if taking on a life of their own. As for his manner of dress, adorning his stocky figure were a formal white shirt, a faultlessly ironed sky-blue evening jacket and matching trousers. He also wore a navy-blue necktie, and a neatly folded white linen handkerchief was visible from his jacket top pocket. In short, the impression he gave off was that of a windswept quail on its way to a dinner party.

Unsure of what to do, I knew I had three possibilities: to withdraw, to step out into the light or to stay as I was. My reasoning was thus: if I stayed as I was I would buy myself some time but hardly resolve anything; If I withdrew, he might think that I was intimidated by him – an outcome I by all means wanted to avoid, whereas if I stepped out into the light and faced him openly, he might interpret my move as confrontational, particularly if he were of a more sensitive nature, as one might expect from a person with such an unusual appearance. I finally concluded that the least painful solution for us both would be if I stayed exactly as I was, but, clumsy and uncoordinated as I am, only seconds later I somehow managed to shuffle out into the light completely.

Much to my surprise he reacted immediately. He jolted as if woken from a deep sleep and darted towards the pedestrian crossing bearing the sign 'Beware! Construction Work Ahead'. He must not have noticed it, since in all the urgency and alarm he tripped over a large chunk of broken asphalt, plummeted to the ground head first and landed on his palms and knees, staining his sky-blue trousers with the granular black asphalt remains. The expression that formed on his face after he rose to his feet and realized that his immaculately clean trousers were now adorned with two unsightly symmetrical stains resembling the Rorschach inkblot test was that of utter horror and bafflement. He was so distraught by this unfortunate incident that he seemed to have forgotten I had ever existed. Seemingly determined to attend to the problem as quickly as possible, he ran to the other side of the street – his dishevelled hair blowing in all directions – and vanished from view. The only thing he left behind was a silvery cloud his warm breath had painted on the canvas of cold air.

As much as I was confused by the event, I was now certain of one thing: he was looking at me after all! But why, I wondered. I knew he could hardly have been moved by my interpretation of the ascending scale of B-flat minor... What was it about me, then, that had caught his interest? Then suddenly it dawned on me. Was it possible that I was as hideous in his eyes as he was in mine? Could it be that the individual standing by the second-storey window of 16 Ostrom Street on this brisk March morning was, in fact, a terrible sight to behold?

Having continued to ponder this potential revelation, I stepped into the bathroom and took a good look at the figure standing before me in the mirror. It belonged to a pitiable and neglected half-creature, a parody of a man. The crimson letters on the T-shirt, which read Punk Is Not Dead, seemed to dominate the image, as if attempting by gravity to keep my slouching, rickety frame in one piece and to ensure its flaccid limbs didn't disperse into the cosmos. Further north, the bright-red strands of peroxide-fried hair and shiny metal objects in the ears seemed a mocking contrast to the lifeless, watery eyes and drooping eyelids.

The figure I saw in the mirror that day made me realize that it had been a while since the mask I so persistently wore reflected my inner state of being, and I concluded it was high time I changed my image.

When I walked out of the bathroom and back towards the living-room window, my eyes became fixed on a detail that I had not noticed before. In the middle of the street, among the pieces of broken, black asphalt, lay his linen handkerchief – as white and immaculate as the first snowflake in winter.

The legal system Tobias was obliged to honour considered the death penalty an utterly inhumane measure and did not practise it. In this legal system the equivalent of the death penalty for a man of Tobias's rank was dismissal from official position. However, his was not a position one may acquire by means of education, recommendations or a six-month training course. On the contrary, the journey a man must take in order to attain this type of position tends to be immeasurably difficult and thorny, and a shortcut has yet to be discovered.

Tobias was reminiscing about the ground he had had to cover on his journey – a journey he was rather fond of despite the hardships – when the Prosecutor stepped forward and commenced his address.

'Are you aware, Mr Keller, that the most severe penalty you could face in case of a violation of any article of the Causal Authority Regulations is your removal from the position of Adviser to the Great Overseer?'

'Yes, I am,' responded Tobias after refocusing his attention on the Prosecutor. Although he spoke with dignity, there was a certain bitterness to his words as he finally verbally acknowledged the outcome he feared the most. Tobias could hear his response echo in every corner of Chamber C of the Second Wing.

'Hmmm... I am surprised that a man of your rank would allow himself such an omission,' said the Prosecutor, meditatively stroking his goatee and resting his elbow on the chair of the woman in the reseda-green dress.

'Mr Diodorus, do you have a specific question for Mr Keller or is this simply a rhetorical remark?' the Presiding Officer interjected, who, to Tobias's relief, also seemed somewhat bothered by the Prosecutor's air of self-importance.

The Prosecutor reassumed a professional demeanour and approached the defendant with determination.

'I imagine you have been made aware, Mr Keller – and I ground my assumption on the fact that prior to being appointed adviser you were obliged to sign the document stating that you were in agreement with the Rules of Service – that pursuant to article 98a of the Causal Authority Regulations, as an adviser you have the right to exert your influence on the subject only when referring him to the Guidelines on page 249 of the aforesaid Regulations. One may circumvent the Guidelines and freely exert one's influence only if one possesses an official, stamped approval from the Great Overseer.'

'Yes, I am aware of this,' responded Tobias briskly.

The Prosecutor felt like strangling Tobias Keller because his question failed to provoke in him the kind of reaction he was hoping for. By the time he posed his next question he was circling the room angrily, and his voice assumed a conniving and ironic tone.

'Yet this had somehow slipped your mind at the moment the act took place, isn't that so? At the moment you committed the act and set the trap for the cyclist in the close proximity of the subject Moritz Tóth, you were miraculously deprived of your ability to use sound judgement!'

'I never said it had slipped my mind,' was Tobias's quiet response. It made the Prosecutor come to an abrupt halt and turn towards him.

A deep silence suddenly filled Chamber C of the Second Wing. The Prosecutor stared blankly at Tobias, failing – perhaps not even attempting – to hide his disbelief. He then posed his final question. 'Are you saying that at the moment you committed the act you were consciously violating Article 98a?'

'Yes.'

'Thank you.'

Beaming with delight, the Prosecutor shot meaningful glances at the members of the Disciplinary Committee. To admit to having committed an act was one thing, but to admit to having been conscious of the actual circumstances at the time of perpetration, as well as to intent, was a different matter altogether. The Defendant Tobias Keller seemed an easy target from the onset, but the Prosecutor never could have guessed it would be that simple.

The handkerchief remained in my cabinet for quite some time before I decided to do anything about it. It proudly gleamed opposite Juliska's framed portrait and spitefully rivalled her fine, delicate features. 'Don't worry, Juliska,' I would comfort her, 'just think of the number of times his obscene snout discharged into it all kinds of slimy excrements and how persistently the poor thing needed to be scrubbed and ironed in order to achieve such perfection.' I wanted it out of my sight, but my conscience, along with the fine silk-ribbon embroidery around the edges, prevented me from ruthlessly discarding it in the rubbish or tossing it back out on to the street where I had found it.

Then, one day as I was standing by the window, I caught sight of him again, crossing that very same pedestrian crossing. He was wearing the same suit, the only difference being that this time the warm rays of the sun elegantly reflected off the newly paved asphalt that sparkled like a sea of black onyx, which consequently connoted a little more luck for his sky-blue trousers as there were no broken chunks for him to trip on. It was a quarter to six. I had forty minutes left before I had to leave for the Opera, which would give me more than enough time to rid myself of the linen handkerchief.

I put on my winter duffle coat, armed myself with a pair of dark shades and stuck the handkerchief in my pocket. By the time I reached the bottom of the stairway (the damned lift was always stuck) he was already well ahead, turning the corner onto Bodajk Street. My initial plan, cleverly concocted three storeys earlier, was to catch up with him, kindly address him as 'sir' and hand him the handkerchief without any particular explanation. It seemed the simplest solution. But the longer I trod in his footsteps, watching his erratic gait and the strands of hair that coiled above his head like a nest of enraged vipers, the more intense and nauseating was the feeling the awkward man was leaving in my stomach. I couldn't exactly swear by it, but every so often I thought I could detect a spasmodic twitch of the body, as if the Devil himself had taken control of him. Although revolting, his unusual behaviour had awoken in me a certain level of curiosity that I was unable to suppress, so I continued to follow and observe him – a choice that my rational side relentlessly kept trying to justify with the likelihood that I would eventually find him in a less macabre state and return the damned handkerchief.

Then I lost sight of him in the vicinity of the park on Kossuth Lajos Street. Children and dogs pranced around densely grouped birch trees while their nannies, mothers and masters followed behind – it was easy enough to get swallowed up in the crowd. I scanned my surroundings in an attempt to figure out where he could have disappeared to. The park was encircled by residential homes, except for the grocer's located opposite the bus stop. I peered inside a few minutes later and spotted him standing between a stall of fresh vegetables and a tinned-goods aisle some ten meters from the entrance, studying a tin of stewed fruit. I then did as my instincts instructed, grabbing a trolley and setting off on a leisurely walk through the middle of the shop.

The grocer's was unusually quiet for that time of day, with Sting and Pavarotti softly singing 'Panis Angelicus' in the background – a housewife's idyllic afternoon ambiance. The pleasant atmosphere had a soothing effect on me, and the moment seemed perfect to finally return the handkerchief. I took a shortcut to the meat section with the intention of getting ahead of him, hoping that he would approach me instead of the other way around, but as our encounter was coming closer, there was something about him that began to repell me all over again, and I grew more and more uncertain of whether I was prepared to make contact with him at all. I finally hid behind a large fridge containing fresh meat and in a squatting position watched him through the glass. He headed towards me through the aisles at a pace that would make a snail seem lively by comparison. The cold air from the open cooler slowly penetrated my coat and the many layers of clothing. I was afraid that I would turn into an icicle should he continue at that pace, and I had already started to devise escape strategies when he suddenly stopped in front of the counter with household products, so that from my vantage point his right profile lingered above a pair of plump chicken drumsticks.

'Well, well . . . haven't seen you around in two whole days!' bellowed a woman with perfectly coifed hair who was sitting behind the counter. The man grouchily mumbled something under his breath.

'The usual?' continued the woman behind the counter in an equally cheerful tone, evidently accustomed to his unconventional social manners. Yet, before even giving him a chance to reply, she placed two large plastic bottles on the counter. The bottles contained some sort of liquid, and the label bore a picture of a skull. I must have produced a noise, perhaps even visibly jerked back in surprise, because the man suddenly turned towards me, and I was once again given the opportunity – this time from up close – to encounter his peculiar gaze. I could feel the adrenalin rush through my veins, for it was then that it became clear to me why his stare seemed so enigmatic the first time I laid eyes on him: his left eye, made of glass, seemed to jump out of its socket and charge towards me like a ferocious beast. I handled the situation terribly and ended up making the worst possible move – I pushed the trolley away energetically and ran out of the grocer's as if fleeing from a raging fire.

The Presiding Officer unexpectedly summoned the members of the Disciplinary Committee for a discussion. He had never before presided in a case in which both the identity of the perpetrator and the intent were established during the first session. Perplexed, he was uncertain as to whether there was any point in continuing with the proceedings or if the penalty should be pronounced immediately and the case excluded from the daily schedule for Chamber C of the Second Wing.

The members of the Disciplinary Committee gathered around his massive, solid-wood desk, and a murmur immediately pervaded the room. The murmur was loud enough to make Tobias feel uncomfortable, yet, even though he was making a supreme effort, he could not decipher a single word, as though the Committee members were speaking in a foreign language. Apart from the one female member, there was also a novice – a trainee, from his appearance – who was eagerly jotting down all his observations in a standard-sized notebook, as well as a somewhat older man whose facial expression suggested complete indifference towards the topic of discussion. The man in question was looking away in silence, whether out of lack of interest or in an attempt to avoid the missiles of spit that the Presiding Officer forcefully discharged through his whisper, since, as the last person to approach his desk, he had no other choice but to position himself directly across from the Presiding Officer, whereas the other two Committee members had cleverly assumed side positions moments earlier.

'You may resume with the examination, Mr Diodorus,' concluded the Presiding Officer, having ordered the members of the Committee to return to their seats. Tobias felt relieved at his words. He was well aware that he would have been written off immediately by any other judicial body had facts of this nature been presented, but, on the other hand, no decision would have been too surprising considering that this was not a case like any other, nor was this any ordinary judicial body.

'Thank you, Mr Presiding Officer,' responded the Prosecutor and flashed a broad grin for the lady in the reseda-green dress, revealing layers of plaque which to Tobias appeared thick enough to clog a sink. The woman in the reseda-green dress lacked the courage to smile back at the Prosecutor, but she nevertheless beamed with satisfaction knowing that the continuation of proceedings would grant her the opportunity to resume watching her skilful admirer perform his duties.

Tobias took a moment to contemplate the extent to which her obvious inclination towards the Prosecutor had influenced the Disciplinary Committee's decision to resume with the proceedings. After all, it was highly unlikely that the third member of the Committee – the rather mature and disengaged gentleman – had contributed to the decision-making process, and as for the young trainee, although he clearly did make an effort, his lack of experience would have prevented his opinion from carrying any real weight.

It was a curious question, posed by the Prosecutor, that suddenly pulled Tobias from his thoughts and made him wonder whether he had unintentionally spoken his musings out loud.

'Can you make an assumption as to why that is so, Mr Keller?'

'I'm sorry, I didn't understand the question.'

'Just prior to the discussion between the Presiding Officer and the Disciplinary Committee you confirmed that at the time the act was committed you were aware of the provisions described under Article 98a of the Causal Authority Regulations, which is why I am kindly asking you to do the following: take a moment to imagine the hypothetical situation in which you are dismissed from the position of Adviser to the Great Overseer', the Prosecutor took particular pleasure in mouthing these words, 'and appointed to the position of Lawmaker, and that it is you who must shoulder the weighty responsibility of drafting a set of regulations that governs the destiny of such a great number of people. Can you make an assumption, from that angle, as to why, without previous approval from the Great Overseer, a man in your position has no right to act upon the subject at his own discretion but is only permitted to refer him to the Guidelines on page 249?'

'I am perfectly capable of making that assumption without having to resort to hypothetical scenarios, Mr Prosecutor,' Tobias responded bluntly. 'I assume that the reasoning behind that prohibition is that the free exertion of one's influence or action at one's own discretion entails an unnecessary risk and alleged endangerment of the subject.'

'Alleged, you say? If I am not mistaken, Mr Keller, it seems to me that you are unappreciative of this rule.'

Tobias hesitated, then decided to lash out at everything for the sake of the truth, regardless of consequences. 'The reason I choose the word "alleged" is because I disagree with it.'

'Ah, I see. The defendant, my dear lady and esteemed gentlemen, disagrees with the aforementioned Article 98a,' said the Prosecutor as he bowed his head before the Disciplinary Committee, and all but the third member of the Committee shot a stern look at Tobias.

'And why do you disagree with it, if you would be kind enough to tell us?'

'One of the reasons is that every action carries a certain level of risk. Not to partake in risky deeds – should that be possible at all – implies everlasting inertia.'

'Not if the deed is authorized by a certified approval from the Great Overseer, which, you will agree, would remove the level of risk.'

'Unfortunately, I would have to disagree with you, but since the reasons for my disagreement are multi-faceted and philosophically grounded, I am reluctant to burden either you or the others present and will specify them only if you openly invite me to do so. However, as I am able to foresee the direction in which you are heading with your examination, I shall satisfy your curiosity by saying only this much: since it was very early in the morning, the Great Overseer was not physically present at the official premises, yet an urgent intervention was necessary. By obtaining official approval I would have absolved myself of any responsibility and probably would not be in the position I am in at the moment, but in the time that I would have required to locate the Great Overseer and obtain a freshly stamped document from his secretary, then return with it by hand to the office and submit it to the guard on duty prior to connecting the Extraordinary Activity Device to the faculty of my free will, the cyclist would have long disappeared from the scene and my attempt to intervene would have ingloriously failed.'

'And your urgent intervention, might I add, was of such vital importance that in those early-morning hours you found it fit to abuse your privileged official position, betray the confidence the Great Overseer had placed in you – which, incidentally, should never occur to a Moral Issues Adviser! – and, with premeditation, devised right down to the minutest detail, might I remind the Disciplinary Committee, violate the sacred provisions described under Article 98a by means of connecting the Extraordinary Activity Device to the faculty of your free will and setting a trap for the cyclist in the form of a sizeable egg-shaped pebble!'

The Prosecutor was waving his arms in the air as he spoke, and his affectations aggravated Tobias to such an extent that he ended up saying something that he had planned to say when the time was right, but choosing a far more courteous approach, had the Prosecutor's behaviour not provoked him. 'Every good deed implies a level of premeditation. Otherwise it would be committed unintentionally and as such would not be considered a good deed.'

The eyes of the woman in the reseda-green dress bulged in disbelief, the trainee lifted his gaze from his notebook only to let his jaw drop to the floor, while the Presiding Officer assumed the task of converting their massive reaction into words.

'For goodness' sake, Mr Keller, this time you have really gone too far! Taking the liberty to call such a thing a good deed! And as for you, Mr Diodorus,' he added quickly, 'please do us all a favour and try to control your inclination towards theatrical expression!'

After the dust in Chamber C of the Second Wing had settled a few minutes later, Tobias felt that he had achieved nothing with his candour except for finally attracting the attention of the third member of the Disciplinary Committee. When Tobias unintentionally threw him a passing glance, he noticed that his eyes were already peacefully resting upon him.

On my way home my thoughts drifted to Noémi and her shapely, feminine calves, her red manicured nails and the sweet smell of rose oil she would always leave on the pillow. I wasn't sure what made me think of her after such a long time – whether I was simply trying to block out my memories of the incident in the grocer's or if it was something else – but my motivation was not all that important to me at that moment. What seemed paramount at that particular moment was to find a way to rid myself of those thoughts because my sudden desire for her was beginning to consume me and was producing a powerful sensation in my groin. *Get a grip on yourself, Moritz. She is nothing but a minor detail from your sinful past; a case of bad judgement,* I kept consoling myself as I climbed the steep staircase of my building, my heart pounding in my chest like a drum.

Returning home brought me back to reality, as the moment I walked through the door the clock on the kitchen wall warned me that I was running terribly late for that evening's performance. I managed to get dressed in a record-breaking minute and a half, to iron my shirt in three, and an additional two minutes later I was completely ready to go. I was already standing at the door with my coat on when something compelled me to turn back. I knew what my heart was longing for because it had happened countless times before, so I glanced over the records on my shelf in search of a two-minute inspiration. An elegant black record cover protruded from the neatly piled classical music collection, the same place where I had once kept my old punk records. I took the record out of the pile and, after removing its cover, gently placed it on the record player. When I positioned the needle near the centre, a familiar warmth rushed through my bloodstream like a drug.

'Ah, *La Traviata*,' I sighed. Maria Callas as Violetta at the São Carlos National Theatre in Lisbon, 1958. The distraught Germont pays a visit to the gravely ill courtesan Violetta with the intention of convincing her to renounce her great love, his son Alfredo, in order to prevent the string of calamities his family would surely suffer should word get out about their scandalous affair. I closed my eyes, trying to imagine the stage of São Carlos and match Callas's intense, resonant voice to Juliska's innocent face, but instead of Juliska I saw Noémi – the delicate, translucent skin of her hands as she composes the goodbye letter to Alfredo in black ink; her dark eyes tearing up as she solemnly promises Germont in the libretto 'Dite alle giovine' that she would do what he asks of her and renounce her love. I attributed my obvious obsession to the likelihood that part of me was still shaken by what had happened, as when a pebble is thrown into a calm lake and it creates ripples on the surface that take a while to dissipate before the water becomes completely still again. I had no way of knowing at the time that the exact opposite was true, that my hasty decision to follow the man with a beak for a nose and a bed of snakes for hair would come to represent the moment of no return and that I was never again to come back to that blissful state of mind commonly known as self-delusion.

It is a well-known fact that the Causal Authority Regulations were not designed by the Great Overseer himself. They were drafted on the basis of his original idea by a group of legislative officials known as the Lawmakers. The Regulations represent a code through which all official persons operating under the leadership of the Great Overseer – just like Tobias – would honour his will and implement the principles of his established order.

Tobias Keller did not agree with the Regulations for a number of reasons, and one of them pertained to the actual basis of their existence. How can one truthfully depict the will of someone whose nature one can never fully know? The activities of the Great Overseer made him impossible to track down, and the scope of his duties was so wide that he sometimes had to be in different places at the same time. The notion that the Regulations presuppose, that someone was skilful enough to track him down, thoroughly question him and record all his convictions on paper – a task requiring several days' work – Tobias considered ludicrous.

Rarely did anyone ever see the Great Overseer. Those who believed they had spotted him in the crowd or had caught a glimpse of him in passing considered themselves truly fortunate because they knew that he would soon disappear like a wisp of smoke in the wind. Afterwards they would always ask themselves if it was really him they had seen.

For that reason Tobias never fully understood on what precisely this set of rules was based. For the irony lay in the fact that he knew the Great Overseer better than anyone, being one of only a handful of people who enjoyed the privilege of being his close associate, and yet the individuals to whom Tobias had to answer in Chamber C of the Second Wing deemed it their right to represent his will with no justified claim to authority. They deemed it their right to represent a will that is above the will of all men and perhaps even – thought Tobias as a wry smile tugged at the corner of his mouth – above the will of the Great Overseer himself.

I woke up abruptly from a light and restless sleep. I am not even sure that it would be accurate to define it as sleeping; perhaps it would be more precise to say that I had been awake for most of the time but would briefly fall into a semi-conscious stupor. When dawn finally broke, I stepped outside for a breath of fresh air, hoping to shake off the night gone by.

It was a Sunday. Those keen early risers had only begun to open their gummed-up eyes to the familiar tunes emanating from old transistor radios and the invigorating aroma of freshly brewed coffee, and there was not a living soul on the streets of my small town. It was drizzling. Small drops of rain hitting the rooftops produced a quiet yet distinct sound reminiscent of a xylophone playing a mystical oriental melody through the hum of the wind. As I was stepping out of the building, a flock of black crows flew over the trees in a panic, as if trying to escape an approaching cataclysm, and I noticed a large number of cats hiding under the parked cars as if from some ominous prophecy; only their green eyes could be seen sparkling like emeralds.

It was most certainly an unusual morning. It is said that our inner demons awaken after the night falls; that, as moonlight gently caresses our faces, our deeply buried fears begin to surface one by one, to swell and intensify until they are so firmly imbedded in our conscious self that they become an inevitable force governing our every action. It is also said that the only source of comfort during such moments is the thought of the ephemeral nature of our fears, the knowledge that morning will once again come to the rescue, that all anxieties will subside and that everything we had once feared will seem remote, irrelevant, perhaps even comical. This particular morning, however, lacked that therapeutic quality. This particular morning was wrapped in a veil of mystery and, perhaps, a covert malevolence. The only detail that detracted from the mysticism of my surroundings was my own presence – but then, my presence seemed mandatory, because how certain can we ever really be that a picture has any existence away from the eye of the beholder?

I did not know where I was going. I let my legs carry me, let the rain run down my cheeks, without caring much where I might end up. At one point it dawned on me that the sinister atmosphere surrounding me closely resembled the one that prevails in Puccini's works and foreshadows the tragic twist of plot. Upon reaching the park on the corner of my street I stopped, let my eyes fall shut and deeply inhaled the smell of wet leaves. All of a sudden I found myself in Cho-Cho-San's Japanese garden, and as the breath-taking view of Nagasaki Bay stretched out in front of me, the wind fiercely blew, shook the branches of Japanese junipers and carried the black earth towards the open sea. My escape to the magical world of Giacomo Puccini provided a degree of consolation, however short-lived, for when I opened my eyes again a moment later I caught a fleeting glimpse of something that seemed painfully familiar. I caught sight of a creature so conspicuous that there was no need for me to take one more look to know it was him. But I looked anyway.

He was standing on the opposite side of the street, in front of the old tinsmith's workshop not far from my building, where the road forks towards the Roma settlement. With his hands in his pockets and his head slightly tilted, he stood motionless as a statue; all that was needed to complete the image was a pigeon on his shoulder. I couldn't get a good look at his face, as he was only half turned towards me, but he seemed to be staring at a particular spot on the pavement, absorbed in thought, which is precisely the reason why I have chosen to define his appearance at the time as particularly unattractive and conspicuous. In fact, something about his pose seemed artificial. I could not think of any other reason why his gaze would be fixed on the pavement other than that he was looking for something, yet his unseemly, stiffened pose suggested a sort of bewilderment rather than an active, investigative state of mind. I picked up my pace, pretending not to have noticed him, as well as to be completely indifferent to the drops of cold rain whipping my face. Placing my confidence in something of a guardian angel, I began to repeat under my breath, *Please don't let him notice me, please don't let him notice me*, and only after I had moved past his static eye did I realize that he was actually looking at me. My heart jumped into my throat, charged with adrenalin just like the time our eyes collided in the grocer's, the difference being that now I was certain my fear was justified; after all, I had sense enough to notice that for some peculiar reason our lives were interweaving and that over the course of time our mysterious connection was acquiring certain dimensions of a fatalistic nature. As reluctant as I was to admit it to myself, he and I now had a past, and I had a strange inkling that we would also have a future.

I walked past the nearby bistro and continued towards the settlement, when I suddenly heard footsteps approaching as if echoing and ruthlessly confirming my most recent thoughts . . . *Good God, is it possible . . . is it possible that he is following me?* I didn't dare turn around, in fear of what I might discover. I kept walking at a fast pace, with the clear intention of losing him, but it felt as though the entire time I was wading through thick mud, because regardless of the distance I thought I had placed between us, the sound of the footsteps was growing ever more intense, and my legs, heavy as lead, were starting to betray me.

Upon reaching the Roma quarter, I decided to proceed right through it, naïvely hoping that he would eventually lose faith and give up the chase. I walked past a scrapyard of scattered boxes, past line upon line of laundry hung out to dry, past the stench of stale blood that lingered in the air like a memento of the fight from the night before. The evidence of human presence comforted me. I could hear the distant swearing of an infuriated woman, and even through all her yelling I was able to detect that every so often the footsteps would cease then continue a few seconds later, as though my stalker was occasionally pausing for some reason. For a moment this made me believe that he was near to giving up from exhaustion, until I realized that I was only being misled by false hope, for each time the footsteps would continue they would appear louder and more determined than ever before.

There seems to be a boundary of authority our sensible self dares not cross but instead chooses to give way to its antagonistic collaborator, that hidden part of our nature, which then leaps to the rescue in the form of an uncontrollable inner impulse. I presume it is for that reason that I could not explain, were someone to ask me, why I had stopped so abruptly between a line of towels and a line of socks, turned to face my stalker and looked him straight in the eye.

We stood across from each other about three metres apart, dripping wet in the pouring rain, and it was as though time stood still. It was quite clear that neither of us had the intention of looking away, which meant that I was once again faced with the opportunity to examine his outlandish appearance and all its particulars. As he was standing in that utterly unreal environment looking like a wet rat, an unbelievable scene was unravelling before me: while his right eye remained stationary and expressionless, his left eye revealed an entire spectrum of varying emotions – from initial astonishment through to suspicion and hesitation and finally to downright desolation and despair, as though imploring me not to judge him. I felt a deep yearning to find out what was hidden under the mask of that man, under his extraordinary physical being, his eyes that didn't match, which at the time struck me as a visual paradigm of man's dual nature. I subsequently came to learn that in his case this exceeded the merely visual, and now I can say with confidence that this was an individual governed by contradictions, polarities, a character in perpetual disarray. The compassion I suddenly felt for him produced a feeling of nausea caused by the stinging awareness of my own hypocrisy, for I did not have the slightest intention of reaching out to him with some noble gesture and gratifying all that empathy.

Although my growing curiosity towards him was becoming insatiable, it required significantly less effort to convince myself that it would be best if we parted ways. And it was as though he could read my mind, because he suddenly made a 180-degree turn and vanished from view, leaving me alone again, wondering if it was all but a dream.

Just then, my thoughts were interrupted by the patter of bare feet. A young woman in a nightgown ran towards me to collect the rain-soaked laundry. Shortly after, a toddler in nappies peeked from under one of the sheets, curious to see who was on the other side. The woman took the child in her arms, and I gave them both a disarming smile, which they reciprocated. Feeling a heavy load lift from my heart, I headed home at an easy pace, when a terrifying realization began to dawn on me: the creature had left behind a trail, and what a trail it was! On electrical poles, rubbish bins and the corners of buildings, marking my exact route and rubbing my nose in my earlier compassion and bad judgement. *Moritz, you stupid, stupid man! Fooled once again . . .*

Although he was no longer physically present in the vicinity, numbers, the colour of freshly spilled blood, served as a warning of his omnipresence in my life and lurked in ambush wherever I turned: first a nine . . . then a one . . . followed by a three . . . and finally a big seven, painted on the old birch tree in front of which he had been standing when I first laid eyes on him.

There was only one place I wished to go after such a course of events. The journey there, not the least bit pleasant, dragged on like a year of famine. The rain had penetrated the worn-out soles of my shoes and my icy-cold feet were ripping my stomach in half. The endless chattering of my teeth made my jaw contract in a spasm that spread to my temples like a drop of black ink in water, but at least I drew comfort from the thought that I would soon see her. It was about seven thirty or eight. I pondered the likelihood that she was still asleep, imagining that she had got drunk on Pinot Noir the night before and had passed out on the sofa and that the fabric was leaving a ribbed impression on her cheek. I also considered the possibility that she was not alone; nevertheless, it was worth the risk.

The flat she was renting was housed in one of those ornamented, perfectly contained Austro-Hungarian edifices from the end of the nineteenth century, located on a quiet tree-lined street. Whereas the building is still occupied by families of good standing, a few decades ago flats here were reserved for the élite – high officials and those in influential positions. I often wondered how she could afford a flat at such a location, probably underestimating the amount of money someone in her profession could make.

As I approached the building I was beginning to distinguish the outline of Noémi's balcony and recalled the time I tried to throw myself off it, drunk as a mule, singing 'Drei weiße Birken' at the top of my lungs until Ilka from the fourth floor appeared with a rolling pin and clear instructions from her mistress Frau Kappelhoff to turn me into steak tartare.

There was no laundry on the line stretched across the balcony, and the door to the flat was shut. When I reached the building I rushed up the stairs, suddenly overcome by a sense of panic that I had come in vain, that she was out of town. My desire to see her was so intense that I would have gladly endured a triple serving of beatings from Ilka if only to find Noémi at home.

She appeared at the door sooner than I had expected. She was wearing a light-green kimono with a missing belt, so she had to wrap her arms around her waist to keep it in place. The smell of fried eggs that drifted from the kitchen was a sign that she was alone after all, as she never cooked for customers. I felt relieved at this thought and found it fit to conclude that, with her hair falling freely over her shoulders and wearing not a trace of makeup, she was more beautiful than ever before. *It's been a long time, Noémi...*

She looked at me as if expecting me to justify my unannounced visit. No words could have illustrated the magnitude of my desire, and I had no intention of lying. I simply stood there watching her, creating for myself a sort of overture. The delicate fabric of the kimono permitted my eyes to follow the curve of her hips and breasts and to take notice of her erect nipples, which she unskilfully tried to hide by crossing her arms over her chest under the pretence of the garment's impracticality. This came as something of a surprise, considering the number of times I had seen her nude. My gaze then moved upwards, following the outline of her neck and jaw line. The rain had just stopped, and the sun's first rays timorously penetrated the lace curtains, illuminating her flawless complexion and giving her lips a fresh, rosy tint. The warmth I once again felt in the area of my stomach and below drew me towards her like a powerful force until I came so close that I could see every minuscule pore on her face, every infinitesimal speck and blood vessel. This was when I realized that she actually looked different from how I remembered. Countless tiny, newly formed lines around the eyes had shaped her expression to suggest the sort of inner maturity that can be achieved only through personal affliction and that commands a degree of respect or civilized distance at least.

In line with these observations, a daunting suspicion began to form in my mind that the many blessings of her newly acquired wisdom would hardly encourage dealings with a loser like me. But a mere couple of seconds later, I could feel her sweaty palms around my neck and her warm tongue in my mouth.

Once again Tobias chose not to leave the room during the break. The third member of the Committee – the elderly and rather peculiar gentleman – was the first to return and remained quiet in his seat. His gaze was directed towards the small, high window to his right. Being the only source of natural light in Chamber C of the Second Wing, it cast a pearly white sheen over the right side of his face.

The others walked in a few minutes later. When the Prosecutor appeared, following the Presiding Officer, Tobias astutely observed that his tie was adorned with two white crumbs and that a third crumb – the largest among them and suspended from his beard – performed nimble acrobatics in concert with his movements. The woman in the reseda-green dress followed behind him. She carried herself differently from the way she had before the lunch break, exuding a newly discovered femininity, her walk as poised and delicate as a prima ballerina's. Perhaps, thought Tobias, she had managed to exchange a few words with the Prosecutor in the canteen; perhaps the Prosecutor discreetly but intentionally brushed the edge of his tray against her buttocks while they were standing in line to pay.

When they had all taken their seats, the Presiding Officer invited the Prosecutor to continue where he had left off before the lunch break. The Prosecutor enthusiastically rose from his chair and headed towards the centre of the room. With a full stomach, he was primed to take on new professional challenges.

'What were you doing on the official premises at the break of dawn on 12 March, Mr Keller?' he promptly asked Tobias.

'The same as any other time of day,' replied Tobias. 'I was observing the development of Case 414 on the monitor – in other words, the life path of Moritz Tóth. Following the life paths of my subjects is a fundamental part of my duties.'

'Certainly. But why did you choose to appear at your workstation so early in the morning on that particular day as opposed to any other?'

Tobias needed a moment to evaluate the question in his mind. He was not entirely sure why he had chosen that particular day rather than any other to arrive early, but he was well aware of the reason he had arrived early in the first place.

'I was hoping that an opportunity would arise which would allow me to assist the subject . . . to lend him a helping hand, so to speak.'

The Prosecutor was somewhat surprised by the emotion, if only a hint of emotion, in Tobias's voice. Not only was he puzzled over the origins of such a sentiment but he was also unsure whether Tobias spoke in earnest or merely in pursuance of a strategy devised during the break to win the sympathies of the Disciplinary Committee. It seemed of crucial importance to the Prosecutor that he establish the correct scenario so that he would know which card to lay down, but, unfortunately, tuning in to the emotions of others was something at which he had never been adept.

'You say that you wished to lend the subject a helping hand,

and I trust we have all been made sufficiently familiar with the fact that this opportunity did indeed finally present itself, as we are with the particulars of the so-called assistance you provided. But do you not consider it vain on your part to exert your influence on the subject freely and at your own discretion rather than by directing him to the Guidelines on page 249 as dictated by the Regulations?'

This was the question the Prosecutor finally decided to pose to Tobias by reason of his natural aptitude for taking the offensive.

Tobias could not believe he was being lectured on vanity by the Prosecutor.

'I have already specified one of the two reasons why I do not believe in Article 98a of the Causal Authority Regulations with regards to inertia. The other reason is that by freely exerting his influence, the adviser imposes his will on the subject to a far lesser degree than if he were to direct the subject to the Guidelines on page 249. The adviser's free exertion of influence through the Extraordinary Activity Device is restricted to the physical circumstances on the ground – or on the scene, if you will – and the decision on how the subject will adapt his subsequent actions to those circumstances is left to the subject entirely. Such a scenario keeps the adviser from imposing a final solution on the subject as would be imposed had he chosen to direct him to the instructions, which is why I consider my influence on the subject in this case to be far more virtuous than if I had acted in accordance with Article 98a.'

'Virtuous, you say? If I correctly understood the reasoning presented in the Decision to Initiate Disciplinary Proceedings, you were the one who set the trap for the cyclist in the form of a sizeable pebble that caused him to collide with the hydraulic digger.

Hence, you were the one responsible for the fact that the intermediary took notice of something he was never destined to discover, thus imposing your will not only on him but also on the subject Moritz Tóth as the final destination on the path of influence!'

'It was possible, all the same, for the intermediary not to have seen what he saw,' Tobias uttered in a dry and mechanical tone, anticipating the type of reaction his words would provoke.

'Hahaha!' laughed Diodorus uproariously, nearly splitting his sides. 'You truly do amuse me, Mr Keller! Do tell us, how would it be possible for him not to have seen what he saw bearing in mind all that we know about the intermediary? Are you not aware of the fact that the intermediary spends days on end actively searching for that which you essentially handed to him on a silver platter when you performed your unlawful deed?'

'We all have –' Tobias began to explain but was interrupted by the Prosecutor who decisively held up his hand.

'No. Please don't answer that. I already know the answer.'

Then the Prosecutor darted a meaningful look in the direction of the woman in the reseda-green dress and added softly, 'We all have a choice,' after which he once again broke out into wild laughter, flaring his nostrils like a dragon. The woman also laughed raucously, revealing a mouthful of unsightly undersized teeth. Even the Presiding Officer let out a brief chuckle, which Tobias did not like in the least.

And had they all known just how much he did not like it they might not have laughed quite as intensely, and the Prosecutor might not have made so many blatant attempts to corner Tobias and induce him to state precisely what he wished to hear, be it the truth of not.

'There is one more detail that puzzles me, Mr Keller,' continued the Prosecutor after he had collected himself. 'Why did you set a trap for that particular cyclist sporting a blue weather-worn uniform and a matching cap as opposed to some other cyclist? I cannot imagine that he was the only cyclist to ride by the scene that morning.'

'Because I knew that by reason of his professional duties this particular cyclist had to ride by that morning. He rode by nearly every morning, and there was a high probability – although one can never be certain – that he would do the same on that particular morning. I felt that I could rely on his presence at the scene.'

'Yet could it be, by any chance, that you chose the aforementioned cyclist because you knew that on that very morning he was particularly irritable, clumsy and heavy-eyed, just as you knew that the intermediary was a susceptible and easily manipulated individual, and that their exposure to the newly arisen circumstances you had imposed on them could produce only one, highly tragic result – tragic not only for the subject Moritz Tóth but also for all those whom you had placed under your influence?'

The Prosecutor's confident voice gradually rose to a powerful mezzo forte. 'Does this not mean, Mr Keller, that by performing your unlawful deed you had, in fact, robbed those individuals of their free will, leaving them with no alternative but to succumb to your influence?'

Instead of giving an immediate reply, Tobias took the time to revel in the Prosecutor's triumphant expression, anticipating the amount of pleasure he would derive from watching the grin wiped off his face after hearing what Tobias had to say.

'In a similar fashion to that in which you appear to be robbing the members of the Disciplinary Committee of their will by exerting your influence in this case?'

Suddenly every trace of self-satisfaction vanished from the face of the Prosecutor, as did the cheerful look from the face of the woman in the reseda-green dress.

'What are you implying?' asked the Prosecutor anxiously, instantly regretting that he had not taken more precaution and simply changed the subject.

'To put it plainly, I am referring to your awareness that the Disciplinary Committee in its present form is unfit to pass judgement in this case. Any decision reached will rely largely on the opinion of its female member alone – and ever since you entered this room, Mr Diodorus, she has had her once-dispassionate head turned, as never before, by the presence of a man.'

A deadly silence permeated the room, causing Tobias's words to reverberate like detonation waves in the ears of the woman in the reseda-green dress.

'How terribly rude!' were the words that spilled from her lips, and all the blood suddenly rushed to her cheeks. She abruptly rose from her seat and started for the door when the Presiding Officer became involved.

'Mr Keller!' he yelled. 'Just look at what you have done! Have you no shred of decency, enough to refrain from insulting the only lady in our company?'

When the Presiding Officer turned to face the woman in the reseda-green dress, his lips curled into a benevolent grin and his voice became as soft as velvet.

'There is no reason why you should not return to your seat. I am certain that Mr Keller said what he did in a simple outburst and not because he truly meant it. You may rest assured that the absence of your charm and expertise would be ever so apparent to us all and would constitute a considerable loss to the proceedings, which is why I am kindly asking you to reconsider your departure.'

Before he continued, the Presiding Officer darted Tobias a stern and disapproving look. 'And you may also rest assured that Mr Keller will be deprived of his basic procedural rights should he continue with such insults.'

Albeit reluctantly, the woman in the reseda-green dress did as the Presiding Officer had asked and returned to her seat. The Presiding Officer breathed a sigh of relief.

Having been struck by a pang of guilt over his verbal assault, Tobias was glad that the woman had chosen to stay, and he also noticed that the third member of the Committee – the peculiar gentleman – who had earlier let out a few spontaneous chuckles at the woman's fiery reaction, had stopped laughing and turned his attention elsewhere. All the persons present in Chamber C of the Second Wing had calmed down. All but one.

Not only was the Prosecutor still in distress but he was as angry as a wounded snake at Tobias Keller, because he had noticed that for as long as two whole minutes the woman in the reseda-green dress had not once looked over in his direction.

The first time I met Noémi was at Zichy Square on my way home from a medical examination. I recall Dr Horvát – safely hidden behind the impenetrable wall of false concern and the thick lenses of her glasses – informing me about a dramatic 15 per cent loss in body weight since she had last examined me. She asked me if I had been drinking and if I had been following the nutritional regimen she had prescribed, and I responded that, of course, I had not been drinking and, of course, I had been following the regimen with rigorous discipline. Needless to say, it was a bold-faced lie if there ever was one. The truth of the matter was that in the months preceding the examination my life had become drained of all meaning and seemed to be disintegrating in slow motion before my very eyes. I had also managed to acquire a collection of chronic illnesses with dubious characteristics, such as irritable bowel syndrome and non-specific tachycardia. Furthermore, despite all the therapy I was receiving, I still needed my liquor like a newborn needs its mother's milk, and had Dr Horvát been the least bit concerned about my health, instead of merely eager to ease her duplicitous health-practitioner's conscience, she would have noticed that my eyes were nearly falling out of their sockets that morning from vomiting and that my stomach was the size of a watermelon; had she been the least bit concerned, she would have eventually sensed my desperate need for attention, understanding and close human contact, just as Noémi sensed my condition later that day at Zichy Square.

She was standing with two other scantily clad women in the middle of the square, looking my way, and I immediately understood the motive behind her interest. In an attempt to circumnavigate them, I started to cross the street outside the pedestrian crossing, only to be knocked over by a Harley that came flying around the corner, instantly making me land nose first on the pavement. The thick folder I was carrying was propelled to the other side of the street; medical reports, referrals and X-rays took off left and right – my liver in one direction, a kidney in another ... Then this scantily clad but genial girl approached me and kindly helped me collect all my scattered body parts. While discretely inspecting the documents as she gathered them off the pavement, she commented that as far as she could tell it would take a miracle to get me out of the mess I was in. I gave a witty reply about how a new nose and a good beating would do just fine for the moment, which, in hindsight, appears to have been quite an astute observation.

I was lucky enough to end up without any serious injuries – only with some rather profuse bleeding. The young woman who helped me collect my documents suggested we go to her house so that she could disinfect my wounds. She said that she lived just around the corner and that her name was Noémi. I took her up on the offer, mainly because I had little option.

She did indeed live around the corner, right off the square on Naspolya Street, near the kiosk with Csaba's legendary breaded chicken wings. The building had no lift, so we had to climb up the stairs to the third floor. On the landing between the first and second floors we passed a colossal creature in a long black coat buttoned up to the neck who contemptuously measured us from head to foot. Noémi whispered that the creature's name was Ilka and that she was commonly known as Ilka the Minotaur and advised me not to take her scornful grimaces to heart. Upon entering the flat, she led me through the narrow hallway and into the living-room and left me sitting on the sofa while she went to fetch the supplies necessary for the forthcoming procedure. The room seemed to be covered with a sheen of cleanliness and smelled like a bouquet of wild flowers, making me feel like a withered weed by comparison. When Noémi returned with an eager expression on her face and a huge cardboard box overflowing with medical supplies, I suddenly felt like I had not travelled that far from Dr Horvát's office. She sat beside me and rummaged through the box, which was when I noticed that the collection of documents revealing my state of health was lying open for inspection on the table in front of us. I caught her gaze sweeping over it a few times, and that finally gave me the incentive to share with her my sad story.

I told her about Juliska, my great love and later my great loss. I told her about Juliska's unconventional upbringing, about her father the military envoy who dragged her and her sister from one private school to the next in faraway locations such as China and Indonesia. I also told her about something that was very difficult for me to share with anyone, especially with Dr Horvát and her psychiatric team; I relayed to her the details of the fierce argument that had broken out on the day of the funeral between Juliska's father and me in front of their most intimate family circle – he had blamed me for his daughter's demise, saying that had she not met a bum like me she would never have been driving her new

Lexus through that run-down industrial quarter in the dead of night.

Noémi listened with a compassionate expression on her face, occasionally nodding her head in understanding. However, what I did not know as I sat there watching her tend to my wounds was that while patiently allowing me to lift the blackness from my heart for one afternoon she had in mind an entirely different form of therapy, a dose of which I was to receive from her several times a week in the course of the following two months for the considerable sum of seven and a half thousand forints per hour.

After I returned home from Noémi's on that ill-fated morning when I desperately tried to evade the grotesque creature that I later adorned with the nickname 'the Birdman', I was greeted by a deadly silence, and Juliska's portrait seemed to stare at me like an apparition from behind the glass door of the cabinet. Her blue eyes, suddenly turbulent like the sea on a stormy night, inquisitively followed me around the room.

Overcome by exhaustion, I took a moment to rest in my armchair. I could hear water dripping in the bathroom – I knew this to be the tap with the worn-out rubber washer I kept reminding myself to replace – which was when it occurred to me that if there is one thing that I dislike in people, it is inconsistency, when they head in one direction in their aspirations but then retreat to old habits out of sheer laziness.

I once swore that I would not be that kind of person; on the fateful day of my encounter with my grandfather's violin following the dress rehearsal of *Turandot*, I listened to a voice within, followed a sign. I believed in signs. I believed in an idea. I vowed that I would remain true to that idea and follow in my grandfather's footsteps, perhaps become a member of the Opera orchestra or even go a step further and compose something of my own one day. An idea, however, is never born at our own command but chooses to wait for fertile ground – a moment when we are so susceptible to it that we would sacrifice everything for its sake; then it launches into the air like a hurricane, pulling everything else along in its wake.

For this reason, by believing in the abovementioned idea, I was also obliged to hold on to other beliefs which, instead of facilitating the fruition of my original idea, ended up being an aggravating factor. I believed that I could redeem myself for my past mistakes by eradicating not only the visible remnants of my past life which I so persistently wore – the red hair, earrings and T-shirts with provocative writing – but also everything else that I once zealously represented. I believed it to be my duty to honour Juliska by remaining eternally faithful to her and that I could easily obliterate from my mind my last encounter with Noémi with a change in attitude and an unwavering decision. I believed in the necessity of sacrifice for the sake of a higher artistic goal, in the vow of celibacy, in suffering as a solitary act.

Feeling utterly powerless, I let my head drop to my chest, when I suddenly caught sight of the white linen handkerchief, the corner of which was barely visible on the floor beneath the armchair. It must have fallen out of my pocket when I returned home in a frenzy following the failed attempt to return it to the Birdman a few days earlier. I picked it up, and as I held it in my hand the images of recent occurrences came flashing through my mind . . . the skulls on the two plastic bottles, the fixed grin of the obliging woman at the grocer's, the red numbers, the Roma child in nappies, the delicate skin of Noémi's thighs . . . At first I was unable to comprehend how all these events were connected, as if for some reason I lacked the ability to observe the picture as a whole. The one thing I was sure of, however, was that they had managed to fog the image of Juliska and place her on the sidelines of my life. And something was also telling me that these were events over which – even though I was the main protagonist – I did not have much influence.

I spent a moment or so pondering the word influence and began to realize something that had been right in front of my eyes but that I had been too distraught to recognize: that all those events or fragments of events could, in one way or another, be traced back to one central figure – to him. This uninvited revelation made my blood run cold, for it all suddenly started to resemble the work of the devil himself.

My situation at the time was unenviable, to say the least. However, the weight on my heart was gradually lifted in the days to come, for I was finally beginning to understand that my visit to Noémi's was not my own choice but rather the choice of that evildoer who seemed to have led me to her by use of some mysterious force. This realization, incidentally, was a crucial element of my theory about the true intentions of that man – a theory that I developed shortly after and that I will refer to frequently in the pages to follow because it had marked the moment when I began to regard him as the sole source of all my woes.

Tobias was neither the first nor the last adviser to hold deep emotional ties with the case to which he was assigned and the individual whose life path he was required to monitor. Obliged to spend hours on end staring at the monitors, it was the advisers' duty to study the immediate surroundings of their subjects but also to peek into the most intimate areas of their lives. Hence, it was nothing unusual for them to get carried away and aspire to be the ones who – at their own discretion – would salvage their subjects from the blind alleys to which life sometimes leads us, from the emotional dungeons, black holes and other dismal states similar to that in which Moritz Tóth had been imprisoned prior to Tobias's intervention. But unlike many others who had lacked the courage, at the height of his burning ambition to assist the subject in turbulent times, Tobias discovered a source of inspiration as, one morning, he observed a rather specific situation, which led him to devise the perfect plan for turning his fantasy into a reality.

It seemed simple enough. All he needed to do was to connect the Extraordinary Activity Device at the most opportune moment to the faculty of his free will and cause a large pebble to appear – as if out of thin air – into the path of the postman heading out on his morning rounds on his bicycle in the immediate vicinity of the subject. According to Tobias's approximation, the cyclist would in all probability abruptly veer off his path in an attempt to circumvent the aforementioned pebble and dart towards the hydraulic digger, which would be approaching from the opposite direction, thus causing a chain of events that would – herein lies the key to his plan! – allow an odd-looking passer-by to assume the role of intermediary and channel Tobias's endeavour towards the subject as the final destination on the path of influence.

However, this was merely an estimate not a mathematical calculation, and Tobias knew that there was no guarantee that the events would unfold exactly as he had envisioned or that his deed would have the desired effect on the subject. Despite being aware that every action carries an inevitable degree of risk, he had justified his deed on the grounds of being familiar with the subject's character as well as on the grounds of his own good intentions, but he had also drawn motivation from a Socratic instinctive certainty, a kind of heart-felt knowledge. In addition, the fact that the final outcome did not depend on him alone but on the will of all the individuals involved made the endeavour all the more appealing and – as far as he was concerned – all the more just.

Tobias was also aware that similar interventions had been made by advisers in the past, by which they violated the provisions of the Causal Authority Regulations, and that for the most part the proceedings against them had ended to their detriment and they had been permanently replaced from their advisory positions and thus deprived of the opportunity to ever discover the end result their intervention had produced in their subjects' lives. However, despite the serious risks involved, Tobias persevered with his plan with great determination, and in no phase of its implementation was he burdened by second thoughts.

He now showed comparable determination throughout the first day of proceedings, for even though he knew that it was his own fault that the female member of the Committee had nearly left the premises and that his determination would only provide fertile ground for further conflict, he continued to defend his convictions through dialogue with the Prosecutor.

'My mind keeps returning to something you said previously, Mr Keller. You said that it was also possible for the intermediary not to witness what you had imposed on him through your intervention?'

'Yes.'

'It was possible for him not to witness it and to witness it all the same. Correct?'

'Yes, that is correct.'

'How is it possible that after such extensive experience working under the guidance of the Great Overseer you remain completely unacquainted with the concept of anticipation? Have you learned nothing from him?'

'It is illusory to believe that the Great Overseer can foresee an event that relies on the human factor. There is a reason why man was endowed with free will.'

'I would like to discuss with you the principles of free will, as it is a topic of which you seem to be particularly fond.'

The Presiding Officer fidgeted in his chair at the Prosecutor's proposal.

'Mr Presiding Officer, sir, I am fully aware that metaphysical discussions do not fall within the Committee's scope of activity, but I shall illustrate soon enough why it is relevant for this case that I discuss the issue with Mr Keller.'

The Presiding Officer twisted his face into a grimace of reluctant acceptance, and the Prosecutor refocused his attention on Tobias, all the while struggling to uphold an air of determination and conceal the fact that he had lied to the Presiding Officer and that his decision to explore the topic of free will was, in fact, not rooted in any particular plan. Although he could have easily made an educated approximation as to the realm in which it lied, he had the impression that he would have to dig a lot deeper to find the Achilles' heel of Tobias Keller.

'Are you a proponent of free will, Mr Keller?'

'One could say that.'

'A fallible response, you must agree,' was Diodorus's cutting comeback.

Tobias paused. A fallible response to a fallible question, he thought. 'I am a proponent of free will, although my belief in free will is proportionate to my belief in the deterministic order, or predetermination, if you will.'

'Are those not contrasting notions?'

'Precisely.'

The looks of suspicion on the faces of most of the people present gave Tobias a reason to elaborate. 'Dualities coexist all around us. In the physical world we have matter and antimatter, the positive and negative electric charge, quantum mechanics and its wave-particle duality of light and matter; in the perceptible world we have day and night, light and dark, water and fire. Why then is it so difficult for human beings to fathom the coexistence of metaphysical dualities, such as determinism and free will?' For a moment Tobias felt honoured to have been given the opportunity to provide an answer to this question before an audience, as if he were standing side by side with the great David Hume, and he continued, 'Because human comprehension rests exclusively on the faculty of reason, and metaphysics – pertaining to the truth, the absolute and the nature of all existence – is a discipline that delves into spheres beyond mere reason and perception, beyond the known laws of the universe and thus beyond our comprehension.

'In my youth, while on a perpetual search for new knowledge and insight, I would often wonder if there was a straw we humans could grasp at to give meaning to our lives, considering that we are deprived of the ability to penetrate the truths of our existence.

'Then I realized that it all comes down to conviction, or faith, if you will, with which methods of reason share no common ground. And my convictions tell me that if we exclude factors over which humans clearly have no influence, such as the laws of nature, if we exclude situations in which the human being is physically prevented from acting upon their will, then it would be far more beneficial for the human race if each of its members carried within themselves the awareness of the freedom to choose as a birthright or, if they prefer, an inherited burden on their shoulders.'

Tobias paused. There was something else he wished to add but feared that his words would become a target of ridicule by the Prosecutor or even inspire a contemptuous remark. However, the way in which the third and eldest member of the Committee was concentrating on Tobias's elaboration boosted his confidence and instantly removed all hesitation. 'This is precisely the reason why I wished to help the subject. To encourage such awareness in him.'

Surprisingly, no outward signs of ridicule or contempt followed. The Prosecutor continued in an identical tone of voice, choosing to comment on the first, theoretical part of Tobias's account and turning a deaf ear to his sentimental digression into his youth and early reflections, which was perhaps the most cunning, most poisonous approach.

'Hmm . . . how odd this is considering that the provisions in the Regulations are nothing but clear and concise. There is no grey area, there are no inconceivable notions, no unfamiliar ground.'

The Prosecutor slowly walked away from Tobias and towards the back of the room, passing first the woman in the reseda-green dress then the trainee. His hands were clasped behind his back, his fingers mysteriously intertwined, while the hoarse creaking of the old floorboards accompanied his footsteps. Having come to a halt under the beam of light filtering through the small, high window and having thus blocked Tobias's view of the third member of the Committee, the Prosecutor turned around and coldly added, 'And a man who acts in accordance with its provisions is a man with a clear conscience, a man who does not need to question himself and whose mind is not burdened by anxieties such as the one you have just described. This is my own modest conviction, Mr Keller. Do you acknowledge it?'

How very cunning, thought Tobias. He had been listening. 'We all have a right to our own opinion, and it is not my ultimate wish to invalidate the Regulations, but do you honestly believe that everyone who violates one of its provisions deserves to be relegated to a lower position? Is there not a slightest trace of doubt in your mind as to whether such a punishment truly reflects the will of the Great Overseer? Just as any speculation about metaphysical truths is a futile pursuit, it is futile to speculate on the will and nature of any man, figure or entity that is so much greater and so far removed from us. If the world's greatest thinkers, such as Kant and Kierkegaard, were humble enough to acknowledge their limitations, why are you so reluctant to do the same?'

In any other situation, the Prosecutor would have had steam coming out of his ears for having to endure criticism from a deluded fanatic whose vocation consisted of talking hot air – the question is whether he would stand for it at all – but this time he firmly decided to control his anger and let Tobias speak, which is exactly what Tobias did, although not for much longer.

'Mr Diodorus,' he said in a tone that suggested a degree of resignation and fatigue, 'I fear that our lengthy discussion may be testing the patience of the Presiding Officer and the Disciplinary Committee, and I would therefore like to summarize my basic conviction, which is that no one who is governed by laws comprehensible to humanity is bestowed with enough insight to comprehend the laws of the Great Overseer or to know his nature. No one at all.'

Upon hearing Tobias utter these words, the Prosecutor felt as though the fog around him had lifted to make room for a sudden clarity.

'Thank you very much, Mr Keller,' he said, smiling politely.

The discovery that he had an accomplice struck at an inopportune moment. Following a sequence of unanticipated events that culminated in my reunion with Noémi came a period that seemed to ensure a long-awaited respite but ended up causing my ever-so-burdened mind to be raided with additional speculations and deductions. All the clutter I was carrying around needed to be disposed of, but the old wreck of a vessel that was supposed to deliver it to its resting place had trouble sailing in, as though the waves were endlessly throwing it against the rocks.

My continuous contemplation did eventually prove fruitful, but the results were alarming, as all my musings seemed to direct me towards one ghastly conclusion – that the Birdman was planning to wipe me from the face of the earth! This indeed was my theory about the true intentions of that man, and several ominous signs seemed to corroborate my suspicions: the way he stared at my window and followed me to the Roma settlement as though his life depended on it, the red numbers indicating the exact route of my daily activities, the substantial amount of liquid, which I subsequently discovered to be peroxide, evidently intended for removing the traces of blood. It all reeked of premeditated murder, and the words of the accommodating woman at the grocer's who handed him the bottles of peroxide – 'The usual?' – hinted that it was hardly his first time.

One piece of the puzzle, however, was missing, and this was not a peripheral edge or corner piece but a central piece – one that shapes the picture and brings it to life. It was clear to me even then that the missing piece would be the first step towards unveiling the motive, and this missing piece was – the message in the red numbers.

Seven-three-one-nine. This set of seemingly arbitrary figures provoked several questions. Should they be viewed as separate entities or as a whole? Where does the numeric sequence begin, and where does it end? Does the seven mark the beginning and the nine the end or vice versa? Is this a representation of four one-digit numbers, two two-digit numbers or perhaps a combination?

In light of the realization that I had become a target of a deranged mind, I began to feel such repulsion towards the numbers that I could hardly even cast a passing glance at them let alone inspect them in more detail. I could muster only enough courage to face my memory of their obtrusive redness set against the grim backdrop of the rainy morning. This grotesque image produced a dark and sinister ambiance, which was why the entire conundrum surrounding the numbers pointed to a mysterious, esoteric, perhaps even sectarian endeavour. Nevertheless, it could have been any number of things, and, as the situation was becoming far too serious to be left to chance, I had decided on a cunning move – to trick him into reversing our respective roles without him even realizing it until it was too late.

I decided to observe him even more closely than he was observing me in order to find out more and prevent the actualization of his evil plan. Accordingly, I installed one of those five-lever steel security locks and purchased the latest model of Olympus binoculars on which I had to spend half of my savings. For security reasons I decided that I would leave the house only when it was absolutely necessary – in other words, when I had a performance or when I was on assignment.

It was on assignment that I discovered he had an accomplice. There was a nondescript bistro situated on the corner of my street – that very same corner behind which he disappeared after he tripped on the chunk of asphalt and stained his sky-blue suit. With a seating area no larger than twenty-five square meters, a dilapidated tin roof and pork goulash as the only offering on the menu, it was the traditional assembly point for construction workers, local merchants and occasionally Imre, the grumbling postman, in moments of high spirits. I had chosen this particular venue for its strategic position – it was located halfway between his building and mine – as well as the fact that the waiter seemed disposed to allow me to spend endless hours sitting at the corner table by the window, squinting through my binoculars and frantically jotting down my observations in a notebook, all the while sipping on the same cup of tea. He must have thought that I was insane and that it would be best not to engage in conversation with me but to silently accept me as one would a piece of furniture.

It was the dead of the night – the bistro as deserted as a blind alley – when I noticed a sleek man in black enter his building with a briefcase. Somehow I knew he was heading to meet the Birdman – I was more alert than the Devil himself and my instincts were as sharp as a wolf's. Only a couple of minutes later the entrance door opened again, and the two men walked out into the night air.

The gait of the man in black coincided with his appearance –

it was dignified, restrained and perfectly linear, while the Birdman thrust his body left and right like a zigzag stitch, although both were evidently impatient to reach their destination, whatever it may have been. They were advancing quickly towards the bistro, so I quickly reached for a newspaper that someone had left lying open on a nearby table, took cover behind it and poked a small hole in the centre so that I could monitor their movements. The newspaper reeked of cigarette stubs and outdated headlines, and the pallid faces on the obituaries hovered in the air around me.

For me it was a war, a war that was waged the moment I decided to take matters into my own hands. Two distinct types of perpetrator are said to be associated with crimes committed during wartime: the architect of the crime, shielded behind the heavily padded door of his comfortable suburban office and a collection of bureaucratic formalities, and the executor, either bound by the chain of command to act upon the architect's order or else a psychologically submissive individual under the influence of some prevalent ideological or political current.

These two types were precisely what the two men before me began to represent in my eyes. I watched as the contrasting figures walked past the bistro like Dr Jekyll and Mr Hyde; it seemed to be an unimaginable tandem in any other situation but the aforementioned. The Birdman, weak-willed and impressionable, charged ahead frantically like a rampaging beast, while the man in black followed behind him like a shadow, revelling in his cohort's idiocy and maliciously chuckling under his breath at the ingeniousness of it all.

When the two men came to a halt I suddenly felt my relentless devotion to detective work backfire on me. They had stopped in front of my building on the opposite side of the street and were now curiously gazing at my window, as if searching for my silhouette through my late grandmother's lace curtain. Then, at the initiative of the Birdman, they headed in the direction of the red numbers, which was when it all started to go horribly wrong. Upon reaching each individual number, the Birdman circled around it and waved his hands inarticulately, as if he were trying to repel it. It was impossible for me even to speculate on the motive behind such behaviour, but what I found interesting was that his reaction to the numbers spread across a spectrum of sentiments, from compliance to admiration, then fear and ultimately repulsion and resistance. I will remember for as long as I live the expression on his face. With his lower jaw hanging open and his healthy eye rolled way back in its socket, it seemed as though he was about to reach the peak of sexual arousal, that he was so close that, even though he was overwhelmed by humiliation and shame, the poor man simply could not stop. The man in black followed him, mumbling something under his breath, and although he was trying to maintain an air of tranquillity and remain poised, his face appeared redder than the numbers themselves, while he seemed about to explode from all the anger he was repressing. On top of this the street lamps cast a white, macabre light on the entire setting, which contributed to my impression that I had somehow wandered into Antonin Artaud's Theatre of Cruelty.

When the Birdman's behaviour began to border on the fictitious, the man in black had no other choice but to hold down his companion's extremities and forcefully separate him from the numbers. On the way back he addressed the Birdman with a remark that sounded more like a warning than a piece of well-meaning advice, which I happened to overhear through the part-open window in front of which I was sitting. Although his scarlet face suggested that he was still fuming with rage, the warning was delivered in a dry and dispassionate tone that seemed to fit him perfectly.

'Stop pouring oil on the fire, Ezekiel. You might be seen.'

'Does this mean that you also lack insight into the nature of the Great Overseer?'

'I believe my insight surpasses your own.'

'Fair enough. Considering that you are one of his advisers, I have no reason not to take your word for it. So what kind of nature is this then? Would you be so kind as to describe it?'

'It is impossible to describe.'

'Certainly. It would be presumptuous even to attempt to describe his intricate nature in the limited time we have at our disposal. A clear oversight on my part.

'Let us then set aside the topic of his nature. Could you describe his physical characteristics, such as his facial features or the colour of his skin? It seems needless to ask if you have ever seen him . . .'

There was no reason for him to nestle in false hope. It was already clear to Tobias that the Prosecutor's intention was to strike where he was most vulnerable and that there would be no method with which he could defend himself. All Tobias could hope for at that point was to endure the blows stoically and with dignity.

'Not in the traditional sense of the word.'

Upon hearing this, the Prosecutor flinched, feigning surprise, then addressed the Presiding Officer under the pretence of providing a clarification of Tobias's response.

'Of course. Considering that the office is merely a transit point for the Great Overseer as he spends the majority of time in the field, it has been a while since Mr Keller has been granted the opportunity to inspect him closely, rendering him unable at present to provide us with a true description of his features. Yet another oversight on my part.

'But surely there have been occasions when you discussed official matters over the telephone, Mr Keller. Perhaps you could describe his voice to us.'

While Tobias remained silent, the Prosecutor derived great pleasure from watching him sink deeper into the abyss of humiliation with each question posed.

'What about touched? Have you ever touched him, Mr Keller? He must have offered you his hand in passing or tapped you on the shoulder as a sign of appreciation for all the hard work you have been putting in throughout your years of service . . .'

Tobias was silent because he had nothing to say. The Prosecutor knew very well what to say but was silent because it benefited him to let Tobias's humiliation last for as long as possible. When he finally spoke, there was not a trace of forced politeness left in his voice.

'My dear lady and esteemed gentlemen,' he shouted, pointing at Tobias like a scientist at a by-product of some freakish experiment, 'standing before you is an adviser to the Great Overseer, allegedly in close cooperation with him, yet not only has he never heard or touched him he also does not believe in the Causal Authority Regulations!' The Prosecutor snatched the Regulations from his desk and waved it over the heads of the Committee members. 'The more I think about it, I find it reasonable to conclude that Mr Keller meets all the criteria for a diagnosis of schizophrenia. Goodness gracious, could he have made it all up? Mr Presiding Officer, are you certain that Adviser to the Great Overseer is his exact calling? Have you carefully inspected his résumé, compiled by the Personnel Sector and forwarded to you as part of the case documents?'

Although it was unheard of for a Presiding Officer to render accounts to anyone regarding his official activities – especially to a Prosecutor – the man in question was so baffled by the newly established facts as to the vague relationship between the defendant and the Great Overseer that he completely disregarded procedural hierarchy. The Presiding Officer obediently put on his glasses, letting their wide frame comfortably settle into his fleshy cheeks, and embarked on a search for the aforesaid document among the heap of papers on his desk.

'This does indeed seem to be his calling... so it says,' he muttered in a low voice after he had found and examined the document.

'There is no reason to doubt my –' Tobias attempted to explain before the Prosecutor brutally interrupted him with a deafening protest.

'Mr Keller, you are clearly jesting with this Committee! You dare spill philosophical wisdom about the nature of the Great Overseer, yet you fail to give us a single piece of information that would corroborate your communication with him. If you have never seen, heard or touched him, how does he make contact with you? By post?'

'No.'

'Dispatcher?'

'No.'

'A carrier pigeon?'

'No.'

'Have you ever received an official document from him, such as a stamped approval for operating the Extraordinary Activity Device at your own discretion?'

'No, because it was never necessary. The deed that is the topic of discussion here was my first and only such activity. As you are aware, I failed to seek approval for this deed and am subject to these disciplinary proceedings as a result of that failure.'

'Judging by your recent responses I am inclined to believe that you chose not to seek approval because you knew that there was no realistic chance for you to obtain it, unless you finally manage to convince me of the opposite and specify at least one method of your official communication with the Great Overseer. Every employee must receive some form of feedback about his work from his employer. How do you know when he is addressing you, and how do you know that it is you he is addressing rather than someone else?'

'I . . . carry an awareness.'

'What kind of awareness?'

'The kind of first-hand awareness of indisputable value, which since the dawn of mankind –'

'Answer my question. What kind of awareness?' interrupted the Prosecutor.

'An awareness with which each one of us is endowed regardless of –'

The Prosecutor's patience was noticeably wearing thin. His stabbing gaze and bulging neck veins clearly commanded an answer from Tobias.

'What kind of awareness, Mr Keller?'

Tobias's eyelids suddenly grew heavy, and his eyes fell shut, leaving him alone in the darkness, as if buried under the black earth.

'Intuitive.'

Now the Prosecutor had him. 'Esteemed members of the Committee, while the Great Overseer's Adviser for Moral Issues has nothing but intuitive awareness as proof of his alleged communication with his superior, we, on the other hand . . . we have the Regulations.' Having made his point the Prosecutor unceremoniously shoved the Regulations in Tobias's face. Tobias stared at the large bold letters against the pale background of the front cover.

'Black on white, Mr Keller.'

The following day, at the crack of dawn, the haunting sound of his name roused me from a deep sleep and followed me throughout the day like an uneasy conscience, for I could sense his proximity with every step I took – through the squeaking sound of my rubber soles during my usual morning walk, through the high-pitched, presumptuous voice of Mr Kis who called to inform me about the rehearsal schedule, through the screech of the violin strings as the bow mercilessly scraped against them like a blunt kitchen knife. All these sounds seemed to ceremoniously attest to the glory of one unusual name – Ezekiel.

It is said that one is more likely to find inspiration while roaming through dark alleys at ungodly hours of the night, crippled by fear, loneliness, blindness and despair than when endowed with the splendours of a harmonious existence. When out of a dark, remote alley of my soul a melody had formed – a melody as conspicuous as Ezekiel himself – I knew that whoever had said this was telling the truth. I longingly reached for my violin, moved by my own ability to transform my hideous, beaky source of inspiration into an agreeable artistic form.

And what a melody it was! Surprisingly, it was set in a major key and remarkably simple – perhaps even overly simplified from a theoretical point of view – but the emotional gratification it provided was complete and unremitting. It branched out like a tree and echoed ceremonially and polyphonically from every corner of my living-room, as if accompanied by an ensemble of a thousand bells.

It is difficult to keep joyous news to oneself. Gently, I knocked on her door, nearly glued to the frame from exhaustion and trying to get my breath back from running. As my heart pounded and streams of sweat poured down my body, I prayed to God that I would find Noémi at home, that my efforts would not be in vain. I also contemplated what I would say to her, searching for the words that would truthfully describe my emotions, but this presented itself as a task far more difficult than I had initially imagined.

The elongated brass handle gradually lowered, and the door opened to the sweet aroma of rose oil drifting my way. How elegant Noémi looked as she stood there in front of me in her satiny knee-length skirt, a fitted jacket and a string of pearls around her neck … I assumed that she had just returned home from a formal event – perhaps an opening ceremony or a cocktail party – and the thought of it distressed me, although I knew I had no right to be distressed. *Where have you been, you temptress? Did you enjoy yourself? Did you have one Martini too many and laugh in the company of strange men so loudly and heartily that your eyes filled with tears? And when one of your many admirers asked you about your line of work, what story did you concoct?* A vague expression formed on her face – the same as the last time I had appeared on her doorstep uninvited. I wondered about the true emotion behind her expression, whether it was disappointment, disapproval or simply confusion caused by another unannounced visit on my part, completely overlooking the fact that on both of these occasions the man who stood at her door was a different Moritz than the one she knew – a man like any other, in a woollen V-neck sweater and with barely noticeable traces of red dye at the tips of his hair.

When she finally spoke, I could detect in her voice a strange combination of longing and wariness. 'Tell me, Moritz.'

'Strange things are happening to me . . . and good things, too. Strange and good things at the same time, Noémi . . .' I muttered and sighed, reduced to the size of a shrivelled pea, humbled by my awkwardly constructed sentence and the hot beads of sweat that were rolling down my cheeks as I stood before this beautiful woman. *No, Moritz, you cannot allow this visit to turn into that kind of an encounter. You need a friend. Stick to the point.*

'Come in.'

'I'd rather not, Noémi.' I decided not to prevaricate any further and to inform her without delay the reason for my visit. Just as I had opened my mouth to speak, I heard what sounded like hooves approaching in a three-beat rhythmic pattern. I imagined the sound being generated by some monstrous three-legged ungulate, but soon enough Frau Kapelhoff appeared, stiff as a board, in her clumpy wide-heeled shoes, pounding her umbrella resolutely on the floor after every other step – clomp, clomp, CLOMP . . . Her presence made me lose track of my thoughts, and it must have shown on my face.

'Come on in, Moritz. Don't be a child,' Noémi whispered as Frau Kapelhoff walked by with her nose in the air, pretending not to notice us.

Noémi's flat had always been immaculate. One would think it belonged to a pharmacist rather than to a woman with a professional calling as dubious as hers. The only detail that suggested any form of decadence or vice were the bottles of cheap Pinot Noir stacked on the top shelf in the corner of the living-room – she called them the 'fastest road to oblivion' – but as I set foot in her flat that day I noticed that even the wine was gone. The thought crossed my mind that if Noémi no longer had reason to seek oblivion, if she no longer had anything to run from, then this would certainly explain the change I noticed in her during my previous visit.

Without waiting for an invitation, I allowed my perspiring body to collapse on to the sofa, in spite of being aware of the large damp stain I would leave behind the moment I stood up.

'Would you like something to drink? Tea, coffee?' she asked while removing the pearls from her neck and placing them on the table in front of me.

A bottle of Jack would do. 'No, thank you,' I replied.

Then she pulled a chair over from the dining room, pushed the small table aside and sat opposite me, so close that our knees were touching. She posed the following question, and only an honest and straightforward reply could release me from the shackles of her piercing gaze, 'What's troubling you, Moritz?'

To begin with, it was the question itself that troubled me – I had come to her in a moment of inspiration, bearing joyous news, yet she suggests to have detected in my voice an anguish deep enough to be worth the mention. I cannot say that I was aware of any anguish I was experiencing other than what was caused by my insatiable desire towards her. But the truth always seems to appear before our eyes without warning, like a soldier in an ambush, and the words that follow tend to come out uncalculated.

'I created a wonderful melody, Noémi. A melody I could never have dreamed of creating.'

'I'm very pleased to hear that, Moritz,' was her sincere and warm reaction. As much as I had hoped for this particular reaction a few moments earlier, the second it had left her lips it struck me as ill-suited and mundane.

'No, you don't understand . . . it's so beautiful it's as if . . . as if it's not of this world, yet it originated from a ghastly creature. I don't see how this is possible, and I find it all very confusing.'

Noémi took a moment to think before deducing the following. 'If those two statements are indeed contradictory as you claim – that the melody is beautiful and that it originated from a ghastly creature – then perhaps one of them is untrue. Perhaps the melody is not as beautiful as you had initially thought or the creature not as ghastly.'

I was unable to present a single argument that would refute her impeccable line of reasoning, and yet I found the lack of subjectivity in her words disturbing. I suppose that, much like a child takes comfort in its mother's tender embrace, I took comfort in the belief that she would think quite differently were she to lay eyes on that creature or hear my music.

'Noémi,' I insisted, 'that ghastly creature left numbers in front of my house . . . appalling numbers . . . redder than blood and more sinister than evil itself. His name is Ezekiel.'

Noémi flinched. 'Ezekiel, like the prophet?'

Although the name did sound familiar, and I had even assumed that it was of Hebrew origin and that it carried a Biblical connotation, my fundamental lack of religious knowledge prevented me from expanding on this assumption. Seeing that an explanation was necessary, Noémi rose from her chair and headed towards the bedroom. I could hear the drawer opening on the antique wooden dresser in which she kept all sorts of cherished objects and para-phernalia. She returned carrying a lavishly produced, leather-bound book. She carefully laid it on the table in front of me and opened it at the contents page. Centered at the top of the page was the title, Old Testament, printed in a stylized font. At this point I knew that I had indeed been correct in assuming that Noémi's life had changed profoundly during our months apart.

I glanced at the contents. The aroma of rose petals continued to permeate my senses, fusing with the stench of my sweat, and it all reminded me of us – of my sticky palms pressed against her hips, of her lustful gasps. Then I accidentally came across his angular name in the contents and took a plunge into the abyss of hell, for just as my erection was becoming generous the image of his grotesque face flashed before my eyes.

'It seems that neither of us is as we once were, Moritz,' Noémi remarked, as though she had read my thoughts.

'It certainly seems that way,' was my reply.

I opened the first page of the Book of Ezekiel. Skimming through, I noticed it contained forty-eight chapters. Then Noémi posed a question that made my blood run cold. 'The numbers you mentioned . . . what numbers were those, Moritz?'

In the hope that I had finally come across a lead, I began to turn the pages in a frenzy, reading and interpreting the chapters and verses with the relevant numeric combinations. I was completely focused on the book, and had Noémi not let out a quiet whimper, I never would have noticed that I was crushing her bare foot with my shoe. I stepped away and read out chapter 7, verse 19, which seemed the most logical even though its numeric combination did not contain the number 3. The verse, unfortunately, proved itself irrelevant – something about silver and gold – and Noémi agreed. Then I remembered to reverse the numbers and searched for chapter 39, verse 17. I read the following:

> And thou, O son of man, saith the Lord God, say to every fowl, and to all the BIRDS, and to all the beasts of the field: Assemble yourselves, make haste, come together from every side to my VICTIM, which I SLAY for you, a great victim upon the mountains of Israel: to eat flesh and drink BLOOD.

Indescribable is the state of horror in which I found myself after reading that verse, and I shall thus try to illustrate it through an allegorical account. Several words from the verse cut through the air around me like a two-edged flaming sword. As I attempted to evade them, flinging myself left and right, I slipped into a body of water that I knew had not been there before but had appeared out of thin air just to spite me. The water was cloudy and laden with silt, grime and parasites, leading me at first to believe that I had fallen into some sort of a contaminated lake. However, the deeper I sunk, the clearer it was becoming to me that this was not a lake of any sort but a bottomless oceanic pit like the ones I had read about in science-fiction novels. I could detect on the surface the outline of a female figure reminiscent of Noémi's leaning towards me. Although I desperately tried to reach her, all my attempts were in vain, for I suddenly didn't know what to do with my limbs, as if I had never swum before. The image of the figure progressively deteriorated the deeper I sank, until all that was left was a dark silhouette that could or could not have been human. Then I heard a muted, drawn-out voice calling my name, followed by a tight grip on my hand, which sent shivers down my spine as though I had been shocked by an electric eel. It must have been this sensation that finally tore me away from the state I was in and jolted me back to reality.

Once again I found myself in Noémi's living-room. Abruptly, I pulled my hand away from hers, my greatest concern being to remain lucid enough to make it to the door. I ran down the stairs – I may have even tripped a few times and fallen. Noémi followed me all the way to the front gate, attempting to console me as I headed off down the street.

'Moritz, please don't go. It doesn't have to mean anything . . . It might all just be a coincidence. Moritz, please . . .' until I was no longer in sight.

The course of proceedings against Tobias Keller may serve as a perfect example of how Chamber C of the Second Wing could transform the selfless into the self-indulgent, the humble into the presumptuous, the insightful into the insane. The proceedings held in Chamber C of the Second Wing would distort without exception not only the defendants but also all other participants – the Presiding Officers, prosecutors, members of the Committee – making them the collateral products of some higher mysterious force. Their grimaces would assume unnatural shapes, their reactions would become odd and inappropriate; even the occasional episodes of underhanded humour would vanish entirely. Much like Tobias, other defendants would also initially disregard the horrifying myths they had heard about this place, only to discover halfway through the proceedings that their opinions about Chamber C had changed, having had the misfortune to learn about it from their own experience.

Why did all the people who had ever been under examination in Chamber C of the Second Wing and who had at some point violated the Causal Authority Regulations share the same fate? How many of these people were – like Tobias – driven by honourable intentions? Was their every attempt to present their good intentions to the Disciplinary Committee destined for failure? Does a conflict of convictions always cause a conflict of interest? Is there any hope for Tobias Keller?

Part Two

Part Two

The sound of the mallet against the gong nearly punctured my eardrums, and a multitude of wide-eyed stares emerged from the darkness that had permeated the back rows of the theatre. The intensity of the strike, however, could hardly have been responsible for the audience's reaction, as it was delivered – as in all previous performances – by Boldizsár the emaciated Methuselah. It must have been none other than the daring and venturesome new Calaf, who with his mere presence on stage and a forceful motion of the arm was able to provoke this reaction.

Once the gong resounds ceremoniously, Turandot presents Calaf with the first riddle, 'What is born each night and dies each dawn?' 'Hope,' Calaf replies with confidence. Astounded, Turandot continues, 'What flickers red and warm like a flame yet is not fire?' 'Blood,' Calaf replies, and an expression of shame covers the face of the ice princess. She then poses the final riddle, 'What is like ice but burns?' A silence suddenly permeates the theatre – a silence so thick and absolute that it seems to go on for years rather than mere seconds – until Calaf finally bellows with exaltation, 'Turandot!' Triumphant cheers explode left and right, and an unfamiliar feeling awakens in me, making me wonder, What kind of nonsense is this? How imaginative and intellectually superior would one have to be to respond to those three complex and metaphorical questions with the ease that Calaf just demonstrated? The sensationalism of Puccini's piece was beginning to irk me, and, had anyone told me a few months before that I would feel this way, I never would have believed it.

As it happened, certain unexpected circumstances that had imposed themselves some thirty days before resulted in my more frequent visits to the Opera. In fact, this was due to a violent argument that had erupted between Gorzowski and the young Calaf after Gorzowski walked into the men's room to discover the actor and the prop-man – plus a prop – striking a highly unnatural pose. The incident immediately ended the actor's engagement in the *Turandot* project, and, since there was less than a month left before the next performance, the audition for the new Calaf was announced the following day. The management insisted on being present at each and every audition in order to control Gorzowski's extravagant behaviour and prevent any inappropriate advances or developments, which ultimately left the director with no other alternative but to cast a quick-witted, ambitious and in every sense conventional young man.

With limited time at our disposal we needed to get down to work. We were informed at the outset that rehearsals would take place every three to four days until the new Calaf settled into the routine. Most of my colleagues considered the additional rehearsals a burden, yet for me they were a temporary escape from reality, a chance to postpone the dreaded moment when I would have to deal with the hardships that were waiting at home and face my opponents. I even resorted to taking this a step further and remaining at the Opera longer than was required of me, working on my composition in the orchestra room after everyone else had gone home. On the one hand, there was something therapeutic in knowing that the very same walls within which I rehearsed had witnessed the genius of musicians such as Zoltán Kodály and Béla Bartók, while, on the other, it suited me to be alone with my music, out of harm's way and far from Ezekiel – even if he were the source of my inspiration for the piece – without a worry in the world apart from the creative process. Rózsa the cleaning lady – who, being the last one to leave, would lock up the premises and hand over the key to the guard on duty – would allow me to 'keep her company' while she cleaned up, which would usually take several hours. Rózsa was a plump, cross-eyed but kind-hearted Roma woman, who was in the habit of addressing all the orchestra members as 'child', including Boldizsár, the fossil at the gong. I was grateful to her for paying no particular attention to me or my work. The only time I would be reminded of her presence was when she would sweep around me with her broom or let out an occasional whistle to accompany my composition.

I was deeply committed to the task at hand. I would write and erase, rewrite and erase again, with the goal of eventually rescuing myself from the two principal fears of every artist – anonymity and mediocrity – while at the same time I allowed all other areas of my life to spiral out of control. I was losing interest in the world around me and was beginning to alienate myself from others. Noémi would leave sympathetic messages on my answering machine about the day I tore away from her and fled from her flat, which I would immediately delete and disregard as though they had never existed. I also lacked energy. I would wake up late – something I had never been in the habit of doing – and would often sleep for twelve hours straight without feeling refreshed. If I had used only an additional atom of grey matter, I would have rightfully interpreted this as an indication that things were not quite as they should be.

It was the second and final day of the proceedings. The moment was creeping close for the Disciplinary Committee to hand down the sentence, yet, rather than feeling the slightest bit alarmed, Tobias seemed utterly indifferent to its imminent pronouncement. It was as if it was all happening to some other unfortunate soul who had been forced into assuming Tobias's identity through a physical resemblance, while the real Tobias was given the opportunity to observe the proceedings from a safe distance with dispassionate curiosity. This could have been caused by the combination of two factors: the curious after-effects of yesterday's session coupled with the defendant's state of exhaustion.

The unfortunate soul slouched in his chair, his head falling to his chest like that of a puppet that had been set aside in a dark corner until the next performance. Tobias's attention was so fully captured by the bearings of this mysterious individual that he failed to notice the others present or to catch sight of the document that the Presiding Officer held in his hands. It wasn't until the Presiding Officer began to speak that Tobias lifted his head and realized that the unfortunate soul who had seized his interest was none other than himself.

'Welcome back.'

The document was printed on high-quality double-coated paper with a black decorative border and a recognizable logo at the bottom, the outline of which Tobias was barely able to discern from his vantage point. Such was the paper the Office of the Great Overseer used for its famous 'Reports on the Present State of the Subject', which listed all the current events in the subjects' lives, as well as their emotional state, their joys, thoughts, apprehensions and so forth.

As the Presiding Officer's gaze wandered over the bare walls of Chamber C, he was unconsciously clenching the document in his hands and puckering his lips in contemplation as to how to commence his address to the defendant.

'Mr Keller, I am unsure whether you have been made aware that during the course of the proceedings the Presiding Officer has the right to request from the Office of the Great Overseer a copy of the "Report on the Present State of the Subject" in connection to any case the Office is processing, should there, of course, be a relationship between that specific case and the proceedings led by the Presiding Officer . . .'

Tobias hesitated. On countless occasions had he shared the Office elevator with the courier whose bag heaped with envelopes addressed to various recipients from the Second Wing, but it never occurred to Tobias to link these deliveries with the proceedings held in Chamber C.

'Following yesterday's session,' continued the Presiding Officer, 'which I believe created a degree of confusion and, I dare say, unease among the participants, I decided to request a copy of the "Report on the Present State of the Subject" in reference to Case 414. Because of the nature of the act committed and the circumstances surrounding it, I felt that the Report would significantly deepen the Disciplinary Committee's insight into the psychological profile of subject Moritz Tóth and provide a closer understanding of your decision to commit the act.'

The Presiding Officer was struggling to maintain a composed and official demeanour, and there was no doubt that what he said next had spilled from his lips without his consent.

'Judging from the Report, Mr Keller, I would have to agree with the Disciplinary Committee that the subject's psychological state has become a matter of paramount concern. His sudden indifference towards the world around him – including the amount of time he spends in bed – may be interpreted as an early sign of clinical depression. It would be wise, for the benefit of the proceedings, to examine the extent of your responsibility for his current condition.'

Tobias felt his heart skip a beat, his contented detachment instantly transforming into a feeling of intense involvement and concern. He could hardly bear being uninformed about the development of Case 414 through his temporary removal, and any bad news about the subject Moritz Tóth – particularly resulting from his well-intended deed – he would endure with even greater difficulty.

'Nevertheless, as we are already well into the second day of the proceedings and time is running short, we had better get on with our work instead of leaping to conclusions. Allow me to present the agenda for the remainder of our time together,' was the Presiding Officer's attempt to redeem himself for his carelessness. 'As the Disciplinary Committee and I were summing up the discussion about the "Report on the Present State of the Subject" just minutes before today's session was scheduled to commence, Mr Diodorus appeared at the door, kindly requesting that the session be postponed because of an unexpected family affair he is obliged to attend to. Certainly, we are all aware of how worrisome family matters can be, and, as it is in the interest of the proceedings to have the undivided attention of all the participants, I have decided to comply with his request and postpone the session to ten o'clock. The plan, as it now stands, is as follows. At ten o'clock sharp I shall commence today's session by putting forth to Mr Keller several questions that have arisen from my examination of the "Report on the Present State of the Subject". Then I shall give the floor to Mr Diodorus who – although unfamiliar with the contents of the Report as dictated by the Law on Disciplinary Proceedings – will also be given the opportunity to introduce additional questions should he consider Mr Keller's responses unclear. Following the lunch break Mr Keller will have the opportunity to present his defence, which I imagine he has already prepared. This will be followed by another short recess then the sentencing, after which Mr Keller will be free to return home.'

At that very moment Tobias began to take notice of the people surrounding him, to scan their faces for signs of disagreement with the Presiding Officer's words. The third member of the Committee – the peculiar gentleman – was staring ahead blankly as though deliberately revealing nothing with his expression, which had a detrimental effect on Tobias's morale since he was afraid of losing the man's quiet support in the proceedings. The other two members were focused on other tasks at hand. The young trainee was returning his notebook into his bag with a look of disappointment. The woman in the reseda-green dress was straightening the wrinkles on her garment to make sure her thighs remained fully covered when she rose from her chair, conscious of the fact that in spite of the Prosecutor's burdensome family obligations each of his shamelessly seductive glances was aimed at regaining her sympathies.

There were those who didn't care. But there were also those – a revelation that shook Tobias to the core – who truly believed that things were as simple and straightforward as the Presiding Officer had construed, giving no thought to the possible implications of Tobias's alleged freedom. He felt like shoving his fist into the miniature window or overturning all the furniture in Chamber C out of pure despair, not knowing how else to prove to these people that he would never do anything to compromise the subject Moritz Tóth.

'With the welfare of this man in mind, Mr Keller, I hope in all sincerity that you speak the truth,' remarked the Presiding Officer, which was when Tobias realized that he had spoken his most recent thoughts out loud.

The May Day weekend was just around the corner, and the two-week break we were given before the next performance had caused me to fall into to a state of hibernation. It had rained for days on end – the brisk rain of spring – doubtlessly spoiling the holiday plans of many. The television stations kept reporting that the Danube and the Tisza had both risen to alarming levels and that we could be facing floods that the region of central and south-eastern Europe had not witnessed in a hundred years. I watched rescue teams set up sandbags along the riverbank and other lines of defence – some even in the vicinity of my town. I followed the close-ups of teary-eyed people who had been left without a roof over their heads, but there were also those who had found temporary solace in alcohol and were gleefully floundering through the water and silt. I watched all of these images, secretly wishing that the landslide would come and sweep me away to some remote and far more desirable place . . . *To hell with everything . . .*

I had not seen Ezekiel since the night he inspected the numbers with his accomplice – or, should I say, superior. I cannot say that I went out of my way to look for him, but, nevertheless, I expected his face to emerge eventually from behind one corner or another, as it had done so many times before. But Ezekiel was nowhere to be seen. I wondered what he might be up to, whether the two men had already devised the plan for my execution, when they would release the arrow that they were so consistently aiming in my direction, what my destruction would be like and whether I had the slightest chance of preventing it. After realizing that I had begun to gather dust from lying in bed for so long, I decided to embark on a search for Ezekiel – a move made out of imprudence if not plain boredom, a move that marked what one might call the beginning of the end.

It was early in the afternoon. I thought I could avoid the large drops of spring rain if I carefully chose my route and kept within the dry, sheltered areas under the canopies, balconies and trees, which was why I didn't bother to take an umbrella. My attempt at staying dry, however, did not yield the desired results, and I ended up cursing myself for putting on a brave face. Upon reaching the bistro at the end of my street, I rushed inside to dry off and restore my body temperature with a cup of hot coffee.

The restaurant was swarming with customers. Seated at a couple of connected tables near the entrance was a group of about fifteen young men in blue workers' uniforms, listening to a live radio broadcast of what seemed to be an exciting football match. Sprawled over my favourite corner table by the window were two inebriated idiots who shouted inappropriately over the cheering of the young men and the voice of the sports presenter. Having barely managed to push my way through the crowd, I positioned myself at the bar, turning my back to everyone but the waiter, from whom I ordered a cup of black coffee – extra strong.

I found the waiter's devotion to my order fascinating and utterly inconsistent with the usual treatment I would receive from him. Completely indifferent to the onslaught of demands from impatient customers, he tended to my order as if he had on his hands all the time in the world. The spoon melodiously tapped against the interior of the copper kettle as he stirred the thick, foaming liquid, which he then carefully poured into the cup. On that particular occasion, I must have seemed to him like a flower amid a profusion of weeds – a rare and delicate species requiring special nourishment.

When the coffee was nearly ready, I reached for my wallet in the back pocket of my trousers, and as I glanced over my right shoulder my eyes became fixed on an unusual and rather unattractive sight. Ezekiel's superior – the man in black – was charging down the street with an awkward gait, carrying over his shoulder a large nylon bag filled with what seemed to be sharp, angular objects. His hands were clenched, his jaw tight, his expression grim. He was also listing noticeably to one side, which suggested that whatever he was carrying in his bag was quite a load. When I lost sight of him in the vicinity of Ezekiel's building, I shoved two tatty banknotes in front of the waiter and scurried out of the bistro, leaving behind a resonant slam of the door, a steaming cup of coffee and the waiter's deeply irritated holler, 'What the hell did I make this for then?'

I assumed a position under the old birch tree, which allowed for a perfect view of his two windows. I was hoping to remain unnoticed beneath the thick branches of the tree and to be shielded from the rain, which had, for some reason, often played a role in my contacts with Ezekiel. It was then that I suddenly recalled the moment that I first caught sight of the monstrous creature from my window and how intrigued I was by his appearance. *Oh, how beautifully the tables have turned! Who's watching who now, Ezekiel?*

I knew I was once again a step ahead of them, and I voraciously feasted upon this new state of affairs as I rubbed my palms together and waited for the next thing to happen. Then a vicious wind blew my way, swaying the branches and causing them to swoop very low – nearly hitting the ground – but as soon as they soared back into the air, the view in front of me opened once again, and in one of the windows I spotted Ezekiel's perfectly framed torso.

He was standing at the window completely motionless, as though he had turned to stone. There could have been a number of reasons for this, and I considered it fruitless to engage myself in deeper contemplation of the subject. I assumed that he was expecting his acquaintance – who was running late – but I also could not exclude the possibility that he was simply curious to see if the rain had stopped or if there was a queue in front of the nearby corner shop. All of these prospects seemed more plausible than the possibility that in the shroud of the dismal rainy afternoon he had intentionally sought me out and that through the fierce movement of the branches he was able to spot my unremarkable eyes staring at him.

How I failed in my assumption! I should never have allowed myself the grave error of underestimating him, for, just as I had done so, Ezekiel disappeared from the window, and when he reappeared he sprung a surprise on me – a surprise that served as a reminder of how I always seemed to resort to bad judgement at the most crucial of moments. He reappeared, and in his hands he held a piece of cardboard on which there was a message in capital letters that I couldn't make out from where I was standing. *It is obviously a message, but what kind of a message?* I mused. *Who is it for? Could it be for me? If it is, what does he want to tell me?* I squinted through the intertwined branches, meditating on whether to move closer, but my yearning to read the message was so intense that I suddenly found myself ambushed from all sides by blaring horns and a stream of obscenities, which was when I realized that I was standing in the middle of the street as an obvious target for oncoming traffic. I hurriedly moved on to the pavement, stopping near the tall, wrought-iron entrance to his building. By this time I was as filthy as a sewer rat, with streaks of mud on my trousers as a punishment for the incident I had nearly caused. All I had to do in order to find out what Ezekiel was trying to tell me was to tilt my head back slightly, and this is exactly what I did, even though by then I was close enough to him that I could smell the bad omen as I would rotten meat. His static eye hovered above the sign as I read, as if to underline each individual word:

A CURSE BEHAVES LIKE A LIVE ENTITY. HE WHO FAILS TO RID HIMSELF OF IT SHALL INVITE IT TO MULTIPLY.

The instant I finished reading the horrific message, an elongated shadow arched above him like a claw. I felt my heart leap in my chest, my cheeks burning from the rush of adrenalin, while Ezekiel continued to stand there benumbed, with a hint of sadness in his expression as if a web of ill fortune had spun around his life and he was utterly powerless to free himself. Then a knotted, bone-white hand reached across the window and a curtain of blinds descended over the entire image.

On my way home even the smallest drop of rain – hitting my skin like a razor – exacerbated the anger I was feeling. It would be safe to say that certain sentiments had prevailed to the detriment of reason and had awoken in me a primitive desire for revenge for all the turmoil the two men had caused me. I dare not deny that my next move was radical – I had considered it to be so even at the height of my fury – *but did they alone not invoke the satanic in me, and is it not their own fault that they drew the bow so taut that it snapped before they were able to release the arrow?*

There is, however, a much simpler explanation for my next move – that, quite simply, I was by this time exhausted by the whole affair. I was tired of continuously being thrust into a state of trepidation. I was tired of hiding and of playing the sleuth. I was tired of being consumed with guilt, of moments gone by, and I was also tired of Ezekiel and his partner in crime. But, above all else, I was tired of living my life under overcast skies.

To my great surprise, the first reflection of this new sentiment appeared later that afternoon when the sun finally emerged from behind the clouds and illuminated my birth town with its warm copper glow, at which point I knew that even the most covert forces in the universe had finally allied themselves to my cause rather than that of my opponents.

'Just as I had intuited, an examination of the "Report on the Present State of the Subject" proved to be of indisputable value, allowing me to view the subject Moritz Tóth in a whole new context. Certain details of the Report captured my attention in particular, and I would like to ask you a few questions about them, if you don't mind,' offered the Presiding Officer, eyeing Tobias with expectation, as though genuinely requiring his approval to proceed. Tobias nodded without delay.

'What is the number of cases that you have processed as Adviser to the Great Overseer?'

'For the three years that I have been working in his Office, I have processed a total of fifty-seven cases.'

'What specifically do your duties entail?'

'My principal duty is to observe the life paths of the subjects over the monitor and, on the basis of my observations and the official "Report on the Present State of the Subject", to compile a "Proposal on the Further Course of Action" for each case individually. An adviser is also permitted to operate the Extraordinary Activity Device should he intend to direct the subject to the Guidelines on page 249. Should he, however, wish to exert his influence at his own discretion – as was pointed out a number of times since the beginning of these proceedings – previous approval from the Great Overseer is required.'

'Of which you have only theoretical knowledge, since you considered this specific situation far too urgent to wait for approval – as the law commands – but rather went on to satisfy your unquenchable desire to act at your own discretion by unlawfully setting a trap for the cyclist in the form of an egg-shaped pebble?'

'That is correct, Mr Presiding Officer, sir.'

'You said that your intention was to help the subject by stimulating in him the awareness of the freedom to choose. I assume this means that at the moment of your interference you had reason to believe that he was lacking this awareness?'

'Instead of paving his own road towards achieving his newly arisen ambitions, the subject had acquired the habit of viewing both himself and the world around him through a stereotypical framework, of unjustifiably stigmatizing himself and, most importantly, of assuming the role of a victim. These patterns of behaviour were a major hindrance to his true potential and genius.'

'On this point we agree. But on the other hand, Mr Keller, his behaviour caused no obstruction to anyone nor did it place anyone at risk, which is why I have to admit to being somewhat surprised that you prevented him from doing as he pleased, and even more so if I take into consideration your position on the issue of free will.'

'Any final decision would have been left to him. My sole intention was to interfere with the status quo, to introduce some winds of change, to extend the range of possibilities. Would it have been a better solution if I had chosen to sit with my arms folded? And as far as his lack of interest is concerned, do you not see that even when he refrains from choosing, a person is still making a choice to do so and, with this choice, is moulding not only his own image but also the image of the entire human race? "In choosing myself I choose man," to quote Sartre.'

'I respect your opinion, Mr Keller. Whether or not I share it is a different matter. Now I would like to give the floor to Mr Diodorus,' said the Presiding Officer and turned to face the Prosecutor.

'Mr Diodorus, I understand that as we review the topic of the Report you are faced with the unfavourable circumstance of being forbidden by law to inspect it. However, should you believe that any of the answers provided to us by Mr Keller need clarification, please step forward.'

The Prosecutor rose and approached Tobias with an air of motivation. The Presiding Officer observed a certain fluidity in the Prosecutor's movements and was glad that he had seemed to resolve the family crisis that postponed the session to ten o'clock.

'If I understood correctly, Mr Keller, you wished to encourage in the subject the awareness of his freedom to choose. But can one go so far as to abuse that freedom? What if the winds of change that you had chosen to introduce were, in fact, vicious and vile winds that would induce an act of evil and prompt the subject to commit a sinful deed?'

'That seems a rather far-fetched scenario considering that my intentions were not evil. Those winds had originated from me, and I would be surprised to discover that I am capable of inflicting evil upon another.'

'I beg to differ. I believe that in the course of yesterday's session we were given a perfectly good reason not to be surprised by the notion of a devilish quality lurking in the big heart of Tobias Keller . . . unless the dualities of which he spoke do not refer to him. If I were you, Mr Keller, I would be more careful with what I preach.'

'Mr Diodorus, please adhere to the information available. You are once again basing your arguments on hypothetical situations,' ordered the Presiding Officer impatiently.

The Prosecutor looked slyly at the Presiding Officer, as if to communicate that this was exactly the reaction he was hoping for. 'Hypothetical?' he asked quietly and then continued in the barest of whispers, '. . . then a vicious wind blew my way, swaying the branches and causing them to swoop very low . . .'

As if having taken a slap in the face, the woman in the reseda-green dress gaped at the Prosecutor in disbelief. Most of the participants, in fact, were unable to conceal their astonishment, and as a result of this collective disbelief nobody bothered to second-guess the reason for hers. It went without saying. How fortunate for the lady!

'Mr Diodorus, I am warning you that it is strictly forbidden to reveal details from the "Report on the Present State of the Subject" in front of the defendant.'

The Presiding Officer's chief responsibility in case of a violation of confidentiality was to invest all efforts to prevent any further disclosure of information before the defendant, which meant that he had to refrain from opening the question that was now on everyone's mind. How had Diodorus got his hands on the Report?

The Prosecutor was insolent enough to turn a deaf ear to the Presiding Officer's warning and continue with his misdemeanours. 'And is the summoning of satanic forces in the thoughts of Moritz Tóth indicative of sin? What do you think, Mr Keller? Could the – what did he call it? – radical move he decided to plunge into possibly foreshadow a sinful deed, something he may well regret after the anger subsides?'

This final onslaught of questions made the Presiding Officer's blood boil, and he decided to take measures against Diodorus which, in his twenty-five-years' experience, he had never before taken against a Prosecutor.

'Mr Diodorus, consider yourself dismissed from the proceedings! Even if you are so impertinent as to violate the Law on Disciplinary Proceedings before my very eyes, I would think that you would at least have the sense not to quote the subject's thoughts out of context. And you may be certain that I intend to find out from your superiors exactly how you obtained access to the Report.'

In retrospect, this war of words might best be remembered as the moment when the romance between the Prosecutor and the woman in the reseda-green dress finally took its last breath – a romance that left a permanent scar in the hearts of those it affected during its short lifespan. In the heart of the lady it left a feeling of resentment, because of the mistake for which she knew she could never forgive herself, while in the big heart of Tobias Keller it sparked the growing unease of a man who – only moments before he was due to present his defence – begins to question the ethical value of his actions.

The first thing I did when I got home was reach for the old tin chocolate box on top of the wardrobe. It contained my grandfather's old documents, photographs from his international tours and Juliska's letters. I rummaged through the box, searching for the note with the scribbled address that I had received from Géza Bala, the double-bass player in my grandfather's band. The note was torn off a newspaper that was wrapped around Géza's jam strudel when we met on the pedestrian crossing in front of the town hall. It had been a very pleasant morning, with a jovial Norwegian jazz quartet jiving to a rendition of 'April in Paris'. I repeated the name on the note to myself, allowing it to echo in my mind while recalling the distinctive appearance of the statuesque man with classic facial features, who resembled Cary Grant in his more mature years.

The widely admired Mr Béla Hadik was a close friend of my grandfather. In spite of having come from a blue-blooded family, he lived a life at odds with the trends of aristocratic society. He chose to associate with ordinary folk untarnished by the sugar-coated rules of etiquette – as he liked to call them – and the only indication of his aristocratic background was his passion for hunting small game. Time and again I would find myself reminiscing about our visits to his family estate on Lake Balaton, the succulent roast rabbit in the aromatic herb sauce, the ivory handles on the silverware, the lingering smell of pine trees. Even more vivid is my recollection of the occasional moments when I would sneak out of bed in the small hours of the night, wrap myself in a blanket and sit at the top of the wide marble staircase so that I could eavesdrop on the stories coming from the salon – stories about things of which I had no knowledge, such as adultery, the misconceptions surrounding the then-topical proletarian utopia, as well as something called 'nepotism', to which – as my well-oiled grandfather kept repeating one night – government officials were especially prone.

When I ran into him in front of the town hall, Géza told me that Béla had left the estate as a result of an ownership feud and that he had purchased a flat in Buda, near the Gellért Hotel. We agreed that it must have been a tremendous sacrifice for Béla to leave the family estate, the two of us nostalgically grinning as I reminded him of the bet he and Béla had made – that Béla would one day succeed in convincing the soft-hearted Géza to shoot a pheasant. I asked him if he knew what Béla was up to nowadays, and Géza replied that although Béla did still occasionally go hunting, he had been devoting most of his time and energy to his new hobby of collecting hunting weapons – a detail that flashed through my mind like lightning nine months later. How strange it is that a seemingly insignificant piece of information can fundamentally alter the course of a person's life.

With the lilacs, magnolias and roses in full bloom, springtime in Buda was a true festival of colours and scents. The address on the note had led me to an elegant, cream-coloured villa surrounded by vines and resting in a yellow-rose garden. Near the front gate hung a metal plate with a stylized inscription that read: 'Welcome to the Amália Bed and Breakfast'. Given that the bed-and-breakfast was on the ground floor of the two-storey villa, I concluded that Béla must be living on the floor above. As I was approaching the villa I noticed two overweight, casually dressed women with belt bags also heading in the direction of the gate, so I hurried towards them to prevent the gate from slamming shut. I climbed up the stairs and halted before an ornate double door. I duly rang the bell, and a few seconds later the door opened.

'May I help you?' asked the man in loafers and a towelling bathrobe.

A waft of cool air greeted me from the flat. Probably because of the hot temperature outside, the curtains were drawn over all the windows, and the face of the man addressing me was half obscured in darkness.

'Did I wake you?' I asked sheepishly.

The man gave no reply. I could sense his curious gaze fixed on me, and then he started to approach me until the morning sun – penetrating through the elongated stained-glass window above the staircase – illuminated his face. It was the handsome face of a man well-advanced in years, slightly thinner and more pallid than I had remembered it, but it was, without a doubt, the face of Béla Hadik.

'Moritz, is that you?' he asked with apprehension.

Before I was given a chance to respond, a controlled but excited cry of welcome spilled from his lips. Being pulled into his embrace, I hung over his shoulders, reluctant to reciprocate the affection for fear that my emotions would spiral out of control and that I would end up pouring my soul over his neat-looking loafers.

'You've changed . . .' he concluded after releasing me from his embrace. 'Come in.'

The moment I stepped inside Béla drew the curtains open,

allowing bright light to illuminate the antique furniture in the spacious living-room. I settled on what might be called a divan, upholstered with chocolate-striped olive green satin.

Béla continued to stare at me, his face revealing utter disbelief at seeing me after so many years, until he finally asked, 'May I get you something to drink? Do you like iced tea?'

Having sat down on the divan, I realized that my knees were trembling in apprehension of the favour I had come to ask. In my mind I cursed Ezekiel and the day I became aware of his existence. My eyes fell on an ebony sculpture spiralling upwards between the divan and a nearby rocking chair. It was a representation of a lanky African woman with an elongated neck, balancing a large jug on her head, and it seemed to perfectly reflect my inner state. I desperately needed a chance to compose myself, a moment or two of solitude, so I accepted the offer of iced tea, and Béla left the living-room.

As soon as he reappeared with the glass in his hand, he showered me with questions. He enquired what had been happening in my life, if I had completed university, what I was doing for a living, whether I was in touch with Géza or old Bodi. He made no reference to my grandfather. He was well aware of how attached I was to him and probably feared that the mere mention of his name might rekindle delicate sentiments. Although he was cautious with his questions, the weight of one particular question he was unable to foresee. He asked if I were married. I told him I had been – I suppose a part of me also must have felt like talking. I told him about Juliska, the humble blue-eyed girl who was brutally taken away from me in the full bloom of our love, about our irrevocable vows. Speaking about her again made me realize that I had presented the identical story to Dr Horvát a year earlier while affecting the same pathos in my voice.

'Life is full of surprises, Moritz. We constantly worry about the hand it would deal us, only to be dealt the one we never expected,' Béla concluded through a heavy sigh and wobbled over to the carved wooden cabinet. I remained slumped on the divan, his remark leaving me at a loss for words, as I never could have suspected that Béla – the man who had once embodied all the qualities I strove for in life – could be suffering a secret affliction of his own.

He walked back from the cabinet carrying a Cuban cigar and a small bladed device resembling a mini guillotine. He carefully removed the cellophane from the cigar, split it in two and offered me half. I declined his offer, which he didn't seem to hold against me. He leaned back in his rocking chair, slowly rolling the cigar between his thumb and index finger, looking forward to savouring it while reminiscing about the good old times in the company of a dear friend. Regretfully, I was about to disappoint him.

'I'm in danger, Béla,' was the first sincere statement that came out of my mouth that morning. Béla lit the cigar half with a match and drew the smoke deep into his lungs, sensing that a serious matter was at hand. 'I am a victim of a conspiracy, and it is a matter of life and death. I wish I could tell you more, but I'm afraid that's impossible – for your own safety.'

On hearing this, Béla gave me an inquisitive look.

'What I'm trying to say is . . . You shouldn't get involved any more than is absolutely necessary,' I added carelessly and prematurely, causing Béla to tighten his jaw and slightly raise his head.

'Have you informed the police?' he asked.

'It's far more complicated than that. The plot was designed by a brilliant and cunning mind and has been conducted in such a way that when observed from the sidelines it seems utterly unconvincing. But herein lies the remarkable skill of those involved, because they have managed to cloak evil in the entrancing elements of the fantastic. If death were to walk through that door at this very moment wearing a black cape, would you take it seriously? No. It is out of the question. No way can the police be involved'.

The expression on Béla's face suggested that my explanation left him dissatisfied, yet this was the most coherent explanation I could offer at the time. He leaned towards me and spoke in a soft, quiet voice. 'Moritz, you know I would do anything in my power to help you . . . You're like family to me. If you're in debt, if you need money –'

'It's not a question of money', I interrupted, 'but of logistics . . . which is why I have decided to ask for your help.'

'You see, Béla . . .' I bravely continued, 'what I need to do is to arm myself. As I already explained, it's a matter of life and death, and I need to take preventive measures and prepare myself for the worst-case scenario. Of course, it is possible that the situation will not develop to my detriment . . . Perhaps an unexpected factor prevents the execution of their evil plan . . . Perhaps they end up making a wrong move, and it backfires on them . . .'

None of what I had said – except for the first, crucial sentence – seemed to reach his ears. Instead, my words remained hovering in the air between us.

Béla's face suddenly grew dark. 'I'm afraid I can't help you . . .' he said, looking away.

A brooding silence fell over the room. Béla gazed out of the window, his eyes blankly following the swaying motion of the lilac branches. Stung by a feeling of shame for having come to visit him on such a dreadful occasion, I sat there on the divan, desperately trying to come up with a way to redeem myself, until Béla unexpectedly broke the silence.

'Do you know how I've been spending most of my time, Moritz?' he asked. His tone was strangely reserved – a tone he had never before used with me – and all the tenderness had vanished from his voice. There was no doubt in my mind that he understood the reason for my visit, which was why his question struck me as both redundant and mocking, like he was trying to rub my nose in the fact that he had refused to help me. I saw no point in gratifying him with an answer.

'Most people consider collecting a hobby,' Béla continued, 'but this is because they fail to realize the value of collected items, which can not be measured in dollars or pounds. There are stories behind these items, you see, and I would even go so far as to call collecting a method of communication, considering that each item is a token of a time or historical era of which you are reminded every time you hold the item in your hands. Come with me. There's something I'd like to show you.'

I followed Béla into the hallway. We walked past the spacious, tastefully decorated dining-room and a few other rooms until we reached an impressive leather-padded door at the end of the hallway. Béla opened the door slowly, and it responded with a quiet squeal. As we stepped into the cool room, I was met by the pungent smell of lacquer. Only enough light had crept in between the thick curtains to allow me to distinguish the rough contours of the objects inside. Béla then flicked the switch on the wall, and a crystal chandelier illuminated an elongated table draped with blue velvet. Arranged on the table in a museum-display fashion was a variety of hunting rifles. The only other furniture in the room was a shelf crammed with books on hunting and a small dresser.

Béla began to circle slowly around his collection, examining each piece in the process. He eventually picked up a rifle from the first row.

'This one belonged to my uncle,' he said, 'the good old Winchester 70. It's what I call a field vehicle among hunting rifles – robust in appearance but, in my opinion, one of the most reliable models.'

He placed the rifle back on the table, took a few more steps around his collection then halted again.

'And this stylish-looking rifle you see here', he explained, brushing his fingertips over the detailed silver engraving on a rifle in the third or fourth row, 'is a Kentucky flintlock, famous for being one of Davy Crockett's weapons of choice. It belonged to a wealthy estate owner from Pennsylvania.'

Béla resumed walking around the table and admiring his collection. The next time he stopped, it was to pick up a small pistol. He looked me straight in the eye – for the first time since bringing up the topic of hunting weapons – and said pointedly, 'This, my dear Moritz, is an excellent weapon. The .22 calibre Colt Woodsman, one of the few revolvers officially used in hunting.' He handed it to me, and I noticed that it was heavier and cooler to the touch than its appearance would suggest. 'For those of us who are accustomed to heftier models, this revolver seems like no more than a toy, but, as I am sure you know, appearances can be deceptive. Being so small and easy to manoeuvre, it is ideal for woodland areas and high-density terrain and is typically used for hunting small game, fast-moving targets.' As he uttered these words, Béla clasped his hands together, spread his fingers into a fan and made them flutter like a bird in flight, which instantly brought Ezekiel back to mind, causing me to cringe at the thought.

'I purchased it quite recently from an American diplomat, for my own enjoyment rather than the collection, to be honest,' he explained. He took the revolver out of my hands and placed it back on the table. 'I obtained all the necessary documents, although I haven't had the chance to try it out. I have been planning to visit an old friend in Békés, but whenever it comes down to actually going, I somehow end up lacking resolve. I even bought the bullets . . .' he added, pointing towards the ammunition box.

'There is one thing, Moritz, that every hunter needs to keep in mind.' His eyes softened, and he was once again addressing me with paternal affection. 'Not every moving object is a hunter's prey, nor is a hunter's prey every creature that fits the description of the target, and power is very easily abused. Sometimes just knowing when to spare your prey is a skill more valuable than the ability to kill or capture it. Such knowledge is what distinguishes a real hunter from an amateur. Having said that, I have to admit to being something of a pessimist, believing that this is not a skill one can learn but something that comes from within – an understanding you either have or you don't. If you don't, may God be with you.'

His lecture ended in the same way that it had begun, without warning, and we returned to the living-room. Béla let out a long sigh as he settled comfortably into his rocking chair. He lit the other half of the cigar and began to rock back and forth while absently gazing at the swaying leaves. Silence permeated the room once again. It was as if we had never left our seats, as if our visit to the rifle room had never taken place.

Although I had been convinced that I understood the direction in which Béla was heading with his lecture, I left his flat that day feeling like I had achieved nothing.

I didn't know where to go or to whom to turn. To the left of Béla's door was a narrow flight of stairs that led up towards the attic. I climbed a few stairs and sat down, requiring a moment of solitude before returning outdoors amid the cheerful tourists and the profusion of colours and scents. I sat there daydreaming about Erzsébet Szántó accepting the role of lead soprano in one of my operettas featuring the wondrous melody I had recently created as the main motif. I imagined my name being listed in textbooks of future generations of the Liszt Conservatory as a composer whose unusual arrangements and daringly dissonant chord progressions achieved a revolutionary breakthrough on the Hungarian opera scene by tailoring opera to the demands of modern man.

I didn't hear him come out; he was so quiet. He simply appeared outside the door wearing a linen suit and a wide-brimmed summer hat. The thought instantly crossed my mind that it would be horribly embarrassing if he were to notice that I was still there, and all he needed to do was to turn his head slightly to the left. But he never did.

It all happened very quickly – he didn't even lock the door before heading down the stairs. And yet, there was a definite precision to his footsteps – a rhythmic consistency indicative of resolution rather than urgency. Then, mere seconds before he would vanish from view, I thought I saw him casting a glance at me from the corner of his eye; better yet, it was something I would have sworn he did.

This was the moment when all the pieces fell into place. I stood up and headed back into his flat.

Two days later, when the whole ordeal was over and done with, I paid Béla another visit. While he was in the kitchen brewing a pot of coffee, I slipped out of the living-room to return the revolver. The least I could do to express my gratitude was to obey his rules of the game, because as far as he was concerned – and me, too, as a consequence – our visit to the rifle room had never taken place.

The defence that Tobias Keller gave was unsurprisingly short and concise. Atypically for Tobias, however, he presented the reasons for committing the act in the past tense and with a hint of reflective sadness in his voice, as one might expect from a penitent man, while at the same time appearing to be somewhat estranged from his words.

He claimed that in the moments preceding the act he had recognized an opportunity to assist the subject by exerting his influence in a way that would preserve the subject's autonomy to a maximum degree, even if that implied a violation of Article 98a of the Casual Authority Regulations. As he went on to cite the reasons for his deed, he was guided by the conviction that no code or set of instructions – including the Regulations – is fit to define the boundaries of man's moral competence and that no deed induced by such a code alone is capable of reaching the heights of humanity of a deed that originated from the unique symbiosis of man's two primary inheritances: the graceful perseverance of the heart's innermost sentiments and the expansive power of the will.

Tobias could have added more in his defence, but whenever he opened his mouth to speak, the sight of the Prosecutor's empty seat assertively facing the bench would prevent him from elaborating further.

I placed the revolver in the most visible spot – on my bed, its steel compactness sinking deep into my lightweight apricot-coloured duvet. It appeared so peaceful, so content, as if it were asleep, and I hoped that I wouldn't have to wake it, that by means of civilized conversation I would be able to prevent a tragic outcome of events and circumnavigate the evil fate I shared with Ezekiel.

That day I wore my black corduroy suit over a neatly ironed shirt, as if any possible sins I might commit would be forgiven if I dressed nicely enough. I assumed a position by the window and waited. The silence dragged on, and, although it did occur to me to break it by putting on one of my records, I knew that I had to maintain the highest degree of composure and that I simply could not risk an emotional outpouring. I turned on the radio and tuned to a station with light-hearted Italian tunes featured between newsflashes.

The eleven o'clock chime on the radio had long since resounded when I saw the man in black rush down the middle of the street. In fact, he was advancing at such speed that I didn't even get a chance to sneak out of his field of vision. He noticed the light in my window and threw me a hateful glance.

I was not afraid. I was actually glad that it would all end soon, that I would be a free man released from the horrific shackles they had placed on me. I was also pleased when I noticed him cross over to my side of the street, and when he eventually disappeared from sight I remember thinking to myself, *So be it, let him come to me, let him administer the first blow; that way I can say that I acted in self-defence.* All of a sudden I heard a loud pounding noise and assumed that he was already at my door, until I realized that the noise was coming from outside. Even if he had decided to come to me, he must have changed his mind along the way, because shortly afterwards he reappeared on the street and continued at the same quick pace in the direction of Ezekiel's building.

The moment had finally come for me to make my 'grand entrance'. I gently took hold of my sleeping companion and headed out the door, grabbing the white linen handkerchief from which I was hoping to finally liberate myself on the way. As I already explained, I was not afraid – truly I wasn't – it was the uncertainty that was troubling me. Was there a realistic chance that I could outsmart my opponents with a tactful approach and good negotiating skills? Would I ultimately be forced to resort to my own reflexes and similar primitive mechanisms? How would I handle this? As was the case whenever Ezekiel was involved, it was impossible to predict.

Feeling somewhat unsure of myself, I headed down the stairs and emerged into the cool night air. I turned around to close the door to my building, then hesitated. Under the dim light of the streetlamp, something about the door seemed different. There was something to which my eyes were not accustomed, but I couldn't put my finger on it as all its components were doubtlessly in place – its wooden frame, the decorative stained glass panel at the top, the aluminium doorknob. Then I took a step back to observe the picture as a whole, which was when I noticed that the plate with the number sixteen was missing. Gradually I was able to distinguish the shape of two sixes that replaced it; these, however, were not red sixes but pale-grey, gothic-style sixes, carved into the façade. Ezekiel's superior must have removed the plate as he was passing by, which would account for the noise I had heard just minutes before.

I could suddenly feel a band of pressure tighten around my head, and one of my back teeth cracked as a result of my jaw-clenching anger. I lowered my gaze – the gun in my right hand was as alert as a tiger poised for attack, waiting for me to give the sign. With a tight grip on my steel companion, I allowed it to guide me as I soared through the sleeping neighbourhood like a phantom. I rushed up the stairs of Ezekiel's building, impatient to use the gun on them, already imagining the pair of them drowning in a pool of blood.

On reaching the flat I pounded on the door. The door opened, and I seized the man who opened it by the collar, pulled him towards me and placed the gun against his temple. The stench of an old – albeit hardly unclean – man filled my nostrils. His wilted body, pressed against mine, was starting to give off warning signs of danger. His rapid heartbeat made his bulging neck veins pulsate, the pupil of his healthy eye began to widen, his breathing became shallow and fast. We were so close to one another, as though entwined in a lovers' embrace, and I was gradually becoming aware of what I had done, and I could hardly recognize the actions as my own.

'Make one move and I'll shoot,' I warned the man in black, who was standing in the corner, watching the events unfold.

It was a tiny, spotlessly clean flat. There was hardly any furniture in it – only a bed positioned by the window, a dining-table accompanied by three chairs, a sink and a small refrigerator. Hanging on the wall facing the street were three framed studio photographs portraying a younger, well-groomed and carefree Ezekiel with a boy of about fifteen in a school uniform. I also noticed that there were cartons of pasteurized milk, fruit juice and containers of ready meals arranged on top of the refrigerator, while from the refrigerator door handle hung the empty nylon bag that on that ghastly night the man in black had carried into Ezekiel's flat. I felt great unease at the thought that the food items were, in fact, the angular contents that had been in the bag, whereas a mere ten minutes earlier I would have welcomed this realization.

The man in black caused my attention to shift from the refrigerator when he suddenly kneeled and obediently lifted his hands in the air.

'I said, make the slightest move and I'll shoot!' I yelled. My nerves were as taut as the strings on my violin, and I could feel my confidence plummet. 'Remember, it takes two to carry out your plan, which is why I'm advising you to remain still, unless you wish to be left without your pawn here . . . your dutiful marionette,' I added in a forced tone, desperately trying to sound menacing despite the fact that the sweat that ran down Ezekiel's back was fusing with the sweat that ran down my stomach, that our hearts were beating in a synchronized rhythm, that we were becoming one fragile, indivisible entity.

The man in black addressed our indivisible entity as he remained kneeling on the floor. 'Don't be afraid, Szilveszter . . . don't be afraid. I'll stay still.'

On hearing these words, Ezekiel let out a barely audible squeal. An expression of concern covered the face of the man in black, but he collected himself soon enough and continued in a smooth, measured tone. 'Listen to me carefully, Szilveszter. I have your best interests in mind. Do not move; do not turn your head, do you understand? Just shift your gaze slightly to the right. Can you see what it says? Can you see it, Szilvester?'

Ezekiel timidly shifted his gaze to the right. Following his example, I also looked in that direction and saw on the wall a representation of Jesus Christ in a gold frame – the sphere of healing yellow light generously radiating from his chest. The man in black began to read out the text engraved on a metal plate below the representation.

'Seven is the number of spiritual perfection. There are seven days in a week, seven colours in the spectrum, seven seals of Revelation, seven trumpets . . . one is the number of unity, for there is only one Lord our Father, whose reign is one and whose power is one . . . three is the number of divine perfection, the holy trinity – the father, son and the holy spirit . . .'

These words had a therapeutic effect on Ezekiel. His heartbeat slowed down, and he joined the man in black in reciting the text.

'Nine is the number of spiritual gifts and the number of months that Jesus spent in the womb . . .'

Through a synchronized whisper they repeated the text several times until Ezekiel entered a state similar to the one he was in when he was circling around those same numbers in the street a few weeks previously. His healthy eye rolled back in its socket, and his jaw hung open.

The behaviour that had once seemed so appalling to me I was now, suddenly, seeing in a completely different light. A wave of soothing warmth penetrated my every cell, and our indivisible entity became as light as a petal floating on water. Somewhere in the distance I could hear the sound of waves melodiously crashing against the shore.

'Ezekiel is your name . . . I know it . . .' I uttered.

'If you'd just allow me to explain, you would see that I have nothing but good intentions,' said the man in black. 'But first I would kindly like to ask you to let him go. The poor man is unwell, and all this could cause great harm to his nervous system. Allow me to handle him. You may even keep me at gunpoint the entire time if you so desire. Just allow me to help the man.'

When he said 'gunpoint' I suddenly remembered the crucial role the gun was supposed to play in this encounter. I looked down and noticed that my left hand was still tightly clutching Ezekiel, while my right hand was hanging by my side, as my steel companion – asleep like a hibernating beast – was unintentionally pulling it downwards.

Although I was in no mood to think about defeats, the prospect of victory was no longer bringing me consolation. I asked myself what kind of colossal force I was battling against. Was it against a force whose destructive power was concealed in a feeble shell of an old man? Was it against this other man who was speaking words of compassion while secretly flicking his tongue like a snake? I was no longer sure. I loosened the noose around Ezekiel and remained motionless.

The man in black took hold of Ezekiel and led him towards the bed, leaving me with a sad sense of emptiness. He instructed him to sit down.

'I would like to soak the kitchen rag in cold water,' he said politely. I saw no reason left for me to refuse his request. He walked over to the sink, soaked the rag in water and placed it on Ezekiel's forehead. He then sat beside him and began to speak.

'It's over, Szilveszter. Don't be afraid. Just take a few deep breaths, lean your head on the pillow and try to conjure up in your mind that beautiful hiding place where only you and Tibor are allowed to set foot. If you feel like dozing off, go ahead and do so. Don't fight it. Just go ahead and doze off, Szilveszter . . .'

My understanding of their relationship underwent a radical transformation as I watched this moving scene. With each word from the man in black, Ezekiel – whose bony ankles dangled from the edge of the bed – seemed closer in his mind to his idyllic refuge. When his head finally dropped to the side, the man in black turned towards me and released a long, exasperated sigh. He spoke through a whisper, considerate of Ezekiel who, in a semi-conscious state, was exploring his idyllic setting. The man in black was careful not to disrupt his peace.

'I was afraid that a misunderstanding such as this would arise. I had an inkling, and I had every intention of introducing myself to you and clearing things up. However, certain unexpected events imposed themselves on me, and it was as though all the forces of the universe had united to prevent it from happening.'

I could feel my mouth curl into an ironic sneer, for this was a feeling with which I was very familiar.

Following a lengthy pause, the man in black continued to address me in a particularly disarming tone, making him seem smaller in stature.

'My name is József Varga. I am Head of the Unit for Psychosomatic Disorders at the Ladislas Meduna Psychiatric Institute, and Szilveszter Szabó is my patient of many years.' The doctor's words were coloured by sentiments of inclination towards his patient. As much as he tried to mask these emotions by putting on a collected front, he simply was unable to appear convincing.

'Szilveszter suffers from a type of obsessive-compulsive disorder. In fact, it can be safely said that most people experience mild symptoms of this disorder through minor compulsive rituals induced by superstition, like knocking on wood to prevent bad luck or habitually checking the stove before leaving the house . . .' The doctor smiled as he attempted to introduce a degree of light-heartedness into the conversation, but he quickly reassumed a professional demeanour.

'In the majority of patients, the disorder manifests itself through mild symptoms which, for the most part, cognitive behavioural therapy can keep under control. Nevertheless, we occasionally encounter a more complicated form of this condition accompanied by a complex set of symptoms, as is the case with Szilveszter.'

For a brief moment I turned my attention to Ezekiel, whose trance-like gaze was still wandering around the room.

'Szilveszter, being a highly sensitive individual, falls into the anxious-personality category, and as far as I was able to conclude based on his medical history, his life has always been burdened with mild psychological issues of one sort or another. However . . .' here the doctor took another short pause to choose his words with care '. . . Szilveszter's condition began to deteriorate when he suffered a tragic loss – the loss of his son.'

Although my need to look at Ezekiel had grown even more intense, by this point I did not dare.

'As you may have already concluded,' said the doctor, motioning with his head towards the metal plate on the wall, 'his obsession is a numeric one. His conviction, rooted in the religious symbolism of numbers, is that certain numbers bring good luck and others bad, and he feels a compelling need to focus his attention on the so-called favourable numbers in order to keep his anxiety at bay.

As bizarre as it may sound to us as observers, this numerical fascination is one of the most frequent obsessions associated with this disorder.

'Other than a chemical imbalance in the brain, any stress-provoking situation may trigger the disorder, such as a career change, divorce or, in certain cases, a serious tragedy such as the loss of a loved one. It is somewhat more difficult, however, to establish the reasons why a patient harbours one type of obsession rather than another as well as the factors – whether genetic or environmental – that determine this. Psychoanalysis is still a fairly novel method, discovered at the end of the nineteenth century, and, given that the human psyche is a complex phenomenon, experts still have a long way to go before they discover all of its secrets.

'My psychiatric team, consisting of five doctors, has been struggling for a number of years to understand Szilveszter's case. Keep in mind that psychiatry is hardly an exact science. Finding the appropriate therapy for each patient requires a degree of experimentation and a considerable amount of patience.

'The severity of Szilveszter's illness would vary in a way that was impossible to predict. The winter months went by without major episodes, giving us reason to believe that his condition was finally stabilizing . . . until one morning construction work had caused him to walk through the small street where you live, at which time he noticed something that has been causing havoc in his mind ever since.

'It happened very early, as the first blush of morning rose over the town – so he explained. As part of his morning routine, Szilveszter would visit the local bakery to pick up a loaf of freshly baked bread. However, since construction work had begun on that day or perhaps the day before – he couldn't be quite sure – when he arrived at the main intersection he was greeted by a state of absolute chaos. Workers were arriving from all directions, and some were already setting up restricted-access signs and building-work warnings. When he realized that the street leading to the bakery was also closed off, he decided to take an alternate route and continued through your narrow street, which was still relatively unobstructed.

'No more than a minute or so into his walk, Szilveszter caught sight of Imre the postman approaching from the opposite direction on his bicycle making his morning rounds. Just as they had nodded their heads to greet each other, the postman abruptly veered off his path in an attempt to circumvent a rather large egg-shaped pebble and, having lost control of the bicycle, darted towards the hydraulic digger that was passing by number fourteen. This caused the driver of the hydraulic digger also to veer off *his* route in order to prevent a tragic outcome of events and to drive the digger bucket into the adjacent building at number sixteen – the building in which you live – knocking down the plate with the street number. While contemplating the sequence of events later that day, Szilveszter considered it peculiar that he himself had walked on that same path only a few moments earlier without having noticed the large, perfectly shaped, egg-like pebble similar to those that can be found near the sea, which was why he could have sworn that the pebble had miraculously appeared there for no other reason than to steer the postman in the wrong direction.

'The incident caused a commotion at the building site. A young man of no more than eighteen was operating the hydraulic digger, and the older construction workers – evidently superior to him in authority – kept waving their arms melodramatically and shouting at the poor fellow as he blushed in shame. However, the awkwardness of the moment brought on by a superficial disagreement was, in actual fact, incomparable to the awkwardness and discomfort that Szilveszter was experiencing internally. Although the workers quickly reattached the metal plate to the façade, what had caught Szilveszter's eye the instant the plate fell to the ground was something he could not easily forget.

'To his horror, when the plate with the number sixteen fell off, it revealed the old number that had stood in its place since heaven knows when: the number sixty-six. Given that the building in question was a block of flats rather than a private residence, Szilveszter was well aware that where there were two sixes, there had to be a third one lurking in close proximity, so he took on the task of discovering the identity of the cursed tenant in flat number six, and it was then that this entire nightmare actually began.'

On hearing the word 'cursed', I recalled the ominous message about the curse which the Birdman held up for me the time I saw him standing at the window, and once again I felt a cold chill run down my spine.

'But what about the name, Ezekiel?' I was crouching by now, and the cold wall on which I was leaning was cooling the remains of the sweat that poured down my back.

'As I already mentioned, Szilveszter suffers from a complex form of this disorder, characterized by what psychiatrists sometimes refer to as hyper-scrupulosity. Hyper-scrupulous patients fear that a failure to satisfy their compulsions would lead to a tragic outcome, most typically to the detriment of other people rather than the patients themselves. They tend to assign themselves too profound a role in the fate of others, assuming an unrealistic – or should I say saintly? – responsibility. As unbelievable as it may sound,

Szilveszter was trying to protect you from what is considered the mark of the Devil with numbers he sees as bearers of good luck. As for the name, the prophet Ezekiel was often labelled as having a psychotic personality due to his unconventional behaviour and bizarre rituals – a man of God with strange habits. Ezekiel is the nickname I once jokingly gave him.'

Dr Varga's facial expression seemed to soften as he glanced over at his patient, after which he continued in an academic tone. 'Now that we have covered the behavioural manifestations of the disease, the question that imposes itself upon us is the unavoidable question of cause – where does it all come from? This question has always been a source of great interest to interns at our Institute, although eventually a man of my profession can grow quite tired of it. It seems like with each discovery I make, new ambiguities begin to emerge, reminding me time and again of the complexity of the human psyche and reconfirming my fear that I am unfit to provide a satisfactory answer to this question. Regardless of what is hiding behind Szilveszter's obsession – be it an attempt to redeem himself for a past event which he believes to be his fault or the desire to prevent a similar event from reoccurring – the perception of control unquestionably plays a major role.

'Obsessive-compulsive deeds and rituals often provide the patient with a false sense of control, which is why one type of obsession – particularly if not addressed on time – may also provoke other types. They range from the most benign forms, such as compulsive cleaning or washing of the hands, to those that are far more complex, like compulsions around religious symbolism.'

The doctor surrendered to a lengthy pause. The silence between us granted me enough time to make a connection between the obsessive cleaning he mentioned and the peroxide, turning the unknown into a known factor in an equation that only a few minutes earlier I foolishly thought I had long solved.

He then stooped beside me and continued to speak in a subdued, conspiratorial voice, as if letting me in on a big secret. 'Szilveszter's son was born on 1 September 1973,' he said, indicating with his gaze the metal plate with the same numbers. 'I wouldn't want to jump to conclusions, but I can't help but wonder why he holds those specific numbers in such high regard. Could it be that by repeating them he is commemorating his son?'

The doctor turned towards his patient, and, seeing that he was awake and aware, he started towards him.

'Recently the situation started to get out of hand, so I decided to take radical therapeutic measures. I supplied him with several-days'-worth of food and other basic necessities, strictly forbade him to leave the house and warned him that as Head of the Unit I would make sure that he be denied further medical support from the Institute should he violate the prohibition. However, earlier this evening I received an alarming phone call from him. He was crying into the receiver, saying that he could no longer bear being in the house and threatening to end his misery by turning up the gas stove if he weren't allowed to go outside and find you. I immediately rushed over here. Out of pure desperation – no longer knowing from which angle to approach the problem – on my way over here I removed from your building the plate with the street number so as to reveal the two sixes and brought it to him as proof that you were indeed left to the mercy of chance.'

I don't recall ever having felt like such a fool. Nevertheless, I gathered the courage to approach the bed where they were sitting. I withdrew the linen handkerchief from my pocket and handed it to Szilveszter. By this time I had enough experience with the man to know that he was looking at me, but instead of the expected polarity between his two eyes, his gaze revealed to me something that extended beyond this observation, a new quality that gave warmth and harmony to his expression. What I observed was, in fact, a growing curiosity towards me, as though a mask had been lifted from my face, allowing him to see me for the very first time. I imagined that I was now looking at him in the same way.

'Thank you very much,' he said as he took the handkerchief from me, and this was the first time that I had heard him speak. He hung his head and stared at the handkerchief, gliding his fingertips over the fine embroidery, which was when I seized the opportunity to withdraw quietly with my steel companion, leaving the door open behind me.

The young trainee handed the Presiding Officer the sealed Penalty Decision on behalf of the Disciplinary Committee. When the trainee returned to his seat, the Presiding Officer waited for a formal silence to reign in every corner of Chamber C before he unsealed the Decision and addressed the defendant.

'Are you ready to hear the sentence for the offence you committed, Mr Keller?'

Tobias responded affirmatively, although he could not quite agree with the Presiding Officer's choice of words, for it seemed to him that a state of readiness implied a degree of inner strength which he knew he lacked.

'The Disciplinary Committee', read the Presiding Officer, 'has the honour of informing all persons here present that in the proceedings against Tobias Keller, held in Chamber C of the Second Wing, it has examined all the facts established over the past two days, has compared the particulars of the act committed with the elements of the offence with which the defendant is charged and, based on this comparison, it has reached a final decision on the sentence. After synchronizing the opinions of its individual members, the Disciplinary Committee also concluded that even though under different circumstances the defendant's insistence on his principles and the transparency with which he committed the offence might be considered virtuous, the Regulations are there to be respected, which is why the Disciplinary Committee believes that it would be neglecting its duties if it were to reduce the penalty envisaged by the regulations for this offence. Thus, based on the irrefutable facts which clearly point to a violation of the Causal Authority Regulations and which are listed on the second page of this sentence, but also in view of the obscure relationship which has been proven to exist between the defendant and the Great Overseer, the Disciplinary Committee, comprised of its two distinguished members, has reached the conclusion that the defendant Tobias Keller does not satisfy the criteria for the position of adviser and thus imposes upon him the legal penalty of removal from his official position.'

Tobias had waited like a cocked gun for the final part of the sentence, and it was not until a few moments later that he caught on to the fact that the Committee comprised only two members. In fact, it was a mere coincidence that he registered it at all, because had Tobias's gaze not casually drifted to that supposed third member of the Committee – whose face was illuminated with sunlight filtered through the small high window – and had he not observed that the gentleman's eyes were already peacefully resting upon him, Tobias would never have questioned his own sanity nor would he have wondered whether the curious appearance of the stranger – an appearance that was memorable yet difficult to describe – could explain the uncanny sense of familiarity Tobias had felt towards him from the very beginning. As he deliberated on this further, he came to realize that during the entire course of the proceedings he could not recall any form of communication or interaction between the man in question and the others involved, and it was then that the identity of the stranger suddenly dawned on him.

While this quiet revelation was occurring, to the eyes of the others present Tobias seemed to be observing with keen interest a narrow beam of flickering light that extended to the floor from the tiny window high up in the room to the exclusion of all else. All the Presiding Officer's attempts to inform him that his presence was no longer required fell on deaf ears. The Presiding Officer now resorted to shouting at Tobias in order to make him get up from his seat.

'Mr Keller, you are free to go!'

Tobias flinched at the sudden change of tone, causing the Presiding Officer to feel somewhat guilty for having raised his voice, and this uninvited sentiment, in turn, caused him to embark on an internal monologue about whether he should allow himself to pity the defendant. Although the scales did tip to the defendant's detriment, and although his sudden peculiar behaviour could easily have evoked feelings of compassion in any observer, the Presiding Officer could not help but feel that the defendant had deliberately paved his own way to destruction and that he surely had enough sense to know how futile it is to battle against forces that none of his numerous predecessors were able to defeat.

While Chamber C of the Second Wing could finally allow itself a sigh of relief after having successfully settled yet another case – much like a sovereign would sigh after having crushed an enemy uprising – the Presiding Officer had no choice but to seek on his own the answers to the questions that troubled him regarding the defendant's fate.

Unfortunately, there was no one to tell the Presiding Officer that as soon as Tobias Keller took his first breath of freedom he would begin to engage in an entirely new form of amusement by hiding in remote corners of the building and listening to passers-by whisper fantastic fabrications about Chamber C of the Second Wing.

And there was no way for the Presiding Officer to know that the moment the defendant stepped out of the room and noticed the gaze of his Great Protector still peacefully resting upon him, he would set out down the central corridor of the Second Wing with a lump in his throat and a contrastingly light and graceful gait.

My sleep was rudely interrupted by the unintelligible soliloquy of a wandering drunkard, and I was left feeling broken and disoriented. Like on many previous occasions when I was abruptly awakened, I sought solace in the crisp morning air, the difference being that on this particular morning I walked the streets of my town without turning to look over my shoulder, without noticing suspicious characters lurking around every corner, without watching out for unfamiliar stares, the evil eye, hidden omens or warning signs.

I thought about the one to whom I had ascribed so many foul attributes and derogatory epithets, about how my distorted viewpoint had managed to pollute the image of an innocent man. I could still feel his smell on my jacket and the strands of his hair brushing against my neck. I thought about the incident that had brought us together and wondered in which of the many black holes of my soul I would be residing had our paths not crossed in such a curious manner. It seemed to me that on this particular morning I was once again breathing freely, and, although I was unsure whether I owed thanks to him, a foreign factor or perhaps both, I felt immense gratitude towards the man, knowing that it was none other than his presence in my life that had managed to rouse me from a continuous state of apathy and force me to see things as they really were.

On the way home from my walk, I passed by the red seven painted on the old birch tree in front of building number thirteen. I mustered the courage to approach it, stopping only a couple of metres from the trunk. The red paint had already started to peel off the bark, and when I moved even closer I noticed that it had been applied with an unsteady hand. I recalled the way Ezekiel circled around that seven, the way he held on to the tree, convulsing as though possessed. Then an intriguing thought crossed my mind: how could I be so certain that I have never been the subject of some stranger's scrutiny and that my own behaviour has never caused feelings of pity in another, just like his outlandish behaviour had caused in me? If I alone have been the un-deliberate creator of the tragic fate which I so believed was mine, could I detect a hint of truth in the entire myth about the curse he tried to warn me about? But once I reached my building and was again faced with the two sixes, I recalled the facts the doctor revealed to me the night before, and I quickly dismissed the ridiculous idea. I started up the stairs, laughing to myself at the expense of my fevered imagination . . . *We're two of a kind, Ezekiel and I* . . .

The rest of the day I dedicated to my composition, filling my manuscript with what I considered to be its final version. I had decided to finally take the opportunity after the next performance to introduce myself to Andreas Rusa – the famous pianist, composer and arranger – and kindly ask him to look over my work and assist with any useful suggestions.

When it grew dark I went to see Noémi. I told her that I would be glad of her company and asked if I could spend the night. There seemed to have existed an unspoken agreement between us to postpone the explanation I owed her regarding the unreturned phone calls. She must have intuited that the mysterious occurrences

I told her about had been resolved and that her initial rationale had proved accurate, and she probably wished to spare me any discomfort by being discreet about the issue.

Intimacy of a sexual nature was not on my mind that evening, and all I craved for was her company. It was high time I stopped ignoring the fact that our relationship had grown deeper roots. We spent the evening in front of the television, watching sitcoms and chatting about trivial issues, and I was out like a log with my head on her shoulder in the midst of some Hollywood sob story. In the morning she served us coffee in Nescafé cups she had won as a prize in a contest. With our feet dangling over the ledge and our toes touching casually, we sat on the balcony sipping the coffee, watching our warm breath form various shapes in the cool air and occasionally succumbing to uninhibited laughter for no particular reason.

As I was strolling down Noémi's street on my way home, sleepy-eyed shopkeepers were already busy unlocking the heavy metal shutters of their shops, while some were arranging fruit on the outdoor stalls . . . I passed a tiny bakery just as a young woman was removing a tray of sweet rolls from the oven to place on display by the window. The rolls were steaming hot, with jam oozing out in several places on to the tray.

I entered the bakery, and as I looked up to address the young woman I noticed that she was endowed with an unusual kind of beauty. Her perfectly defined features aside, she exuded an air of grace and contentment – as opposed to someone who spends hours on end standing over hot ovens – which was why I assumed her to be the owner's daughter who was there to provide temporary assistance.

The paper bag in which she placed the sweet roll was so hot that

I had to stretch the sleeves of my sweater over my hands to avoid getting burned. I stepped outside, only to meet her intense gaze on the opposite side of the glass, and I took this as an incentive to return and purchase another roll.

'We wouldn't want to upset the missus,' she commented with a mischievous smile as she gripped a perfectly rounded roll from the middle, arching her slender body over the tray.

Flattered by the attention and even more so by the ingenuity with which she was enquiring about my marital status, I decided to permit myself a moment of harmless flirtation by giving her an honest and straightforward reply, and one which she would also find the most gratifying.

'It's not for the missus . . .' I began, but an unexpected emotion cut me off mid sentence. This emotion could be most closely compared with the acceptable selfishness frequently displayed by children, for much like a child that keeps its arms tightly wrapped around its most precious possession, I had decided to keep the rest of my thought entirely to myself, allowing it to play out silently in my mind . . . *but for a kind of wonder-worker the world has not yet witnessed – the prophet Ezekiel.*

OTHER TITLES IN THE
PETER OWEN WORLD SERIES
SEASON 3: SERBIA

FILIP DAVID
The House of Remembering and Forgetting
Translated by Christina Pribichevich Zorić
Foreword by Dejan Djokić
978-0-7206-1973-7 / 160pp / £9.99

Albert Weisz 'disappears' in his early childhood. To save the young boy from the horrors of a Nazi concentration camp, his father makes a hole in the floor of the cattle truck taking his and other Jewish families to their deaths. He then pushes Albert's brother Elijah and then Albert through and down on to the tracks, hoping that someone will find and take pity on the two boys in the white winter night.

In an attempt to understand the true nature of evil, David shows us that it is necessary to walk in two worlds: the material one in which evil occurs and the alternative world of dreams, premonitions and visions in which we try to come to terms with the dangers around us. With its intricate plot and interweaving of fact and fiction, *The House of Remembering and Forgetting* grapples with the paradoxical and painful dilemma of whether to choose to remember or to forget.

MIRJANA NOVAKOVIĆ
Fear and His Servant
Translated by Terence McEneny
978-0-7206-1977-5 / 256pp / £9.99

Belgrade seems to have changed in the years since Count Otto von Hausberg last visited the city, and not for the better. Fog and mist have settled around the perimeter walls, and everywhere there is talk of murder, rebellion and death.

Serbia in the eighteenth century is a battleground of empires, with the Ottomans on one side and the Habsburgs on the other. In the besieged capital, safe for now behind the fortress walls, Princess Maria Augusta waits for love to save her troubled soul. But who is the strange, charismatic count, and can we trust the story he is telling us? While some call him the Devil, he appears to have all the fears and pettiness of an ordinary man.

In this daring and original novel, Novaković invites her readers to join the hunt for the undead, travelling through history, myth and literature into the dark corners of the land that spawned that most infamous word: vampire.

PETER OWEN WORLD SERIES
SEASON 1: SLOVENIA

JELA KREČIČ
None Like Her
Translated by Olivia Hellewell
978-0-7206-1911-9 / 288pp / £9.99

Matjaž is fearful of losing his friends over his obsession with his ex-girlfriend. To prove that he has moved on from his relationship with her, he embarks on an odyssey of dates around Ljubljana, the capital of Slovenia. In this comic and romantic tale a chapter is devoted to each new encounter and adventure. The women he selects are wildly different from one another, and the interactions of the characters are perspicuously and memorably observed.

Their preoccupations – drawn with coruscating dialogue – will speak directly to Generation Y, and in Matjaž, the hero, Jela Krečič has created a well-observed crypto-misogynist of the twenty-first century whose behaviour she offers up for the reader's scrutiny.

EVALD FLISAR
Three Loves, One Death
Translated by David Limon
978-0-7206-1930-0 / 208pp / £9.99

A family move from the city to the Slovenian countryside. The plan is to restore and make habitable a large, dilapidated farmhouse. Then the relatives arrive. There's Cousin Vladimir, a former Partisan writing his memoirs, Uncle Vinko, an accountant who would like to raise the largest head of cabbage and appear in the *Guinness World Records*, Aunt Mara and her illegitimate daughter Elizabeta who's hell bent on making her first sexual encounter the 'event of the century'. And, finally, Uncle Švejk, the accidental hero of the war for independence, turns up out of the blue one Sunday afternoon . . .

Evald Flisar handles the absurd events that follow like no other writer, making the smallest incidents rich in meaning. The house, the family, their competing instincts and desires provide an unlikely vehicle for Flisar's commentary on the nature of social cohesion and freedom.

DUŠAN ŠAROTAR
Panorama
Translated by Rawley Grau
978-0-7206-1922-5 / 208pp / £9.99

Deftly blending fiction, history and journalism, Dušan Šarotar takes the reader on a deeply reflective yet kaleidoscopic journey from northern to southern Europe. In a manner reminiscent of W.G. Sebald, he supplements his engrossing narrative with photographs, which help to blur the lines between fiction and journalism. The writer's experience of landscape is bound up in a personal yet elusive search for self-discovery, as he and a diverse group of international fellow travellers relate in their distinctive and memorable voices their unique stories and common quest for somewhere they might call home.

PETER OWEN WORLD SERIES
SEASON 2: SPAIN

CRISTINA FERNÁNDEZ CUBAS
Nona's Room
Translated by Kathryn Phillips-Miles and Simon Deefholts
978-0-7206-1953-9 / 160pp / £9.99

A young girl envious of the attention given to her sister has a brutal awakening. A young woman facing eviction puts her trust in an old lady who invites her into her home. A mature woman checks into a hotel in Madrid and finds herself in a time warp . . . In this prize-winning new collection Cristina Fernández Cubas takes us through a glass darkly into a world where things are never quite what they seem, and lurking within each of these six suspenseful short stories is an unexpected surprise. *Nona's Room* is the latest offering from one of Spain's finest contemporary writers.

JULIO LLAMAZARES
Wolf Moon
Translated by Simon Deefholts and Kathryn Phillips-Miles
978-0-7206-1945-4 / 192pp / £9.99

Defeated by Franco's Nationalists, four Republican fugitives flee into the Cantabrian Mountains at the end of the Spanish Civil War. They are on the run, skirmishing with the Guardia Civil, knowing that surrender means death. Wounded and hungry, they are frequently drawn from the safety of the wilderness into the villages they once inhabited, not only risking their lives but those of sympathizers helping them. Faced with the lonely mountains, harsh winters and unforgiving summers, it is only a matter of time before they are hunted down. Llamazares's lyrical prose vividly animates the wilderness, making the Spanish landscape as much a witness to the brutal oppression of the period as the persecuted villagers and Republicans.

Published in 1985, *Wolf Moon* was the first novel that centred on the Spanish Maquis to be published in Spain after Franco's death in 1975.

JOSÉ OVEJERO
Inventing Love
Translated by Simon Deefholts and Kathryn Phillips-Miles
978-0-7206-1949-2 / 224pp / £9.99

Samuel leads a comfortable but uninspiring existence in Madrid, consoling himself among friends who have reached a similar point in life. One night he receives a call. Clara, his lover, has died in a car accident. The thing is, he doesn't know anyone called Clara.

A simple case of mistaken identity offers Samuel the chance to inhabit another, more tumultuous life, leading him to consider whether, if he invents a past of love and loss, he could even attend her funeral. Unable to resist the chance, Samuel finds himself drawn down a path of lies until he begins to have trouble distinguishing between truth and fantasy. But such is the allure of his invented life that he is willing to persist and in the process create a new version of the present – with little regard for the consequences to himself and to others.

José Ovejero's existential tale of stolen identity exposes the fictions people weave to sustain themselves in a dehumanizing modern world.

SOME AUTHORS WE HAVE PUBLISHED

James Agee • Bella Akhmadulina • Tariq Ali • Kenneth Allsop • Alfred Andersch
Guillaume Apollinaire • Machado de Assis • Miguel Angel Asturias • Duke of Bedford
Oliver Bernard • Thomas Blackburn • Jane Bowles • Paul Bowles • Richard Bradford
Ilse, Countess von Bredow • Lenny Bruce • Finn Carling • Blaise Cendrars • Marc Chagall
Giorgio de Chirico • Uno Chiyo • Hugo Claus • Jean Cocteau • Albert Cohen
Colette • Ithell Colquhoun • Richard Corson • Benedetto Croce • Margaret Crosland
e.e. cummings • Stig Dalager • Salvador Dalí • Osamu Dazai • Anita Desai
Charles Dickens • Bernard Diederich • Fabián Dobles • William Donaldson
Autran Dourado • Yuri Druzhnikov • Lawrence Durrell • Isabelle Eberhardt
Sergei Eisenstein • Shusaku Endo • Erté • Knut Faldbakken • Ida Fink
Wolfgang George Fischer • Nicholas Freeling • Philip Freund • Carlo Emilio Gadda
Rhea Galanaki • Salvador Garmendia • Michel Gauquelin • André Gide
Natalia Ginzburg • Jean Giono • Geoffrey Gorer • William Goyen • Julien Gracq
Sue Grafton • Robert Graves • Angela Green • Julien Green • George Grosz
Barbara Hardy • H.D. • Rayner Heppenstall • David Herbert • Gustaw Herling
Hermann Hesse • Shere Hite • Stewart Home • Abdullah Hussein • King Hussein of Jordan
Ruth Inglis • Grace Ingoldby • Yasushi Inoue • Hans Henny Jahnn • Karl Jaspers
Takeshi Kaiko • Jaan Kaplinski • Anna Kavan • Yasunuri Kawabata • Nikos Kazantzakis
Orhan Kemal • Christer Kihlman • James Kirkup • Paul Klee • James Laughlin
Patricia Laurent • Violette Leduc • Lee Seung-U • Vernon Lee • József Lengyel
Robert Liddell • Francisco García Lorca • Moura Lympany • Thomas Mann
Dacia Maraini • Marcel Marceau • André Maurois • Henri Michaux • Henry Miller
Miranda Miller • Marga Minco • Yukio Mishima • Quim Monzó • Margaret Morris
Angus Wolfe Murray • Atle Næss • Gérard de Nerval • Anaïs Nin • Yoko Ono
Uri Orlev • Wendy Owen • Arto Paasilinna • Marco Pallis • Oscar Parland
Boris Pasternak • Cesare Pavese • Milorad Pavic • Octavio Paz • Mervyn Peake
Carlos Pedretti • Dame Margery Perham • Graciliano Ramos • Jeremy Reed
Rodrigo Rey Rosa • Joseph Roth • Ken Russell • Marquis de Sade • Cora Sandel
Iván Sándor • George Santayana • May Sarton • Jean-Paul Sartre
Ferdinand de Saussure • Gerald Scarfe • Albert Schweitzer
George Bernard Shaw • Isaac Bashevis Singer • Patwant Singh • Edith Sitwell
Suzanne St Albans • Stevie Smith • C.P. Snow • Bengt Söderbergh
Vladimir Soloukhin • Natsume Soseki • Muriel Spark • Gertrude Stein • Bram Stoker
August Strindberg • Rabindranath Tagore • Tambimuttu • Elisabeth Russell Taylor
Emma Tennant • Anne Tibble • Roland Topor • Miloš Urban • Anne Valery
Peter Vansittart • José J. Veiga • Tarjei Vesaas • Noel Virtue • Max Weber
Edith Wharton • William Carlos Williams • Phyllis Willmott
G. Peter Winnington • Monique Wittig • A.B. Yehoshua • Marguerite Young
Fakhar Zaman • Alexander Zinoviev • Emile Zola

Peter Owen Publishers, Conway Hall, 25 Red Lion Square, London WC1R 4RL, UK
T + 44 (0)20 7061 6756 / E info@peterowen.com
www.peterowen.com / @PeterOwenPubs
Independent publishers since 1951